No Coward

When a man has nothing left to lose be careful, he can be dangerous, very dangerous – and Olford Tate is now such a man. At the end of a cattle drive from Texas to Missouri, a physician hands the young cowboy a death sentence. His dangerous state of mind results in the cold, calculated killing of a man in front of a room full of witnesses.

When an ageing US marshal with a missing finger and hard-nosed approach to the law comes to his defence, it results in an odd and unlikely partnership. But is Marshal Henry Owens being straight with young Olford or using him for his own purposes? What follows is a treacherous and unpredictable journey as their relationship is tested to the point where there is no room for the coward.

For Armando

For more information about the author
please visit: www.leeclinton.com

No Coward

Lee Clinton

A Black Horse Western

ROBERT HALE · LONDON

ISBN 978-0-7090-9311-4

Robert Hale Limited
Clerkenwell House
Clerkenwell Green
London EC1R 0HT

www.halebooks.com

Typeset by
Derek Doyle & Associates, Shaw Heath
Printed and bound in Great Britain by
CPI Antony Rowe, Chippenham and Eastbourne

1

NOTHING LEFT
TO LOSE

Sedalia, Missouri – 1885

'Doc, I'm, I'm bleeding.' The words came out in a slight stammer between short breaths and with a sense of relief before the cowboy hung his head.

The physician seemed not to notice and continued to write, his eyes cast towards the desk. 'Name?'

The cowboy exhaled with resignation. 'It's Olford. Olford Tate.'

'Olford?' The doctor looked up, questioning, then spelt out each letter. 'O-L-F-O-R-D?'

The cowboy nodded.

'What do you get called? Ollie?'

The cowboy shrugged. 'My mother called me that but Mr Dennison, the team boss, he calls me Ford and the others do the same, most of the time. I like Ford better than Ollie.'

The doctor concealed his smile as he continued writing with care, the nib of the pen scratching its ink on to the small index card before him.

The cowboy watched in silent impatience. 'Doc?' he said at

last, with annoyance.

'Shush,' said the doctor, 'I'm concentrating.'

The young man lifted his eyes skyward to gaze up at the pale-blue pressed-tin ceiling, to study the embossed pattern for a moment or two, as his fingers turned his sweat-stained hat like an upright wagon wheel. 'I'm going,' he mumbled and slid the heel of his boot back towards the chair to stand, scuffing the bleached timber floor.

'You sit. I'm nearly finished,' commanded the practitioner as he laid down the pen, then slowly and carefully placed the card into a little wooden box, between the index tabs marked S and U. 'Done,' he said. 'Now, bleeding, eh? You better get your pants down and let me see.'

The lines on the young man's brow pinched in surprise. 'I didn't tell you where I was bleeding from.'

'No, but it's not a gunshot wound, is it?' The doctor's voice was matter of fact.

'No, of course not.'

'Or a knife wound?'

'No.' The cowboy's tone had a hint of hurt.

'So you must be bleeding in your pants.'

'How did you know that?'

'Men who are shot or cut leak like hell and are mostly lying down but you're sitting up.' The town doctor smiled to reinforce his humour before gently closing the lid of the box. His eyes now engaged the cowboy, who sat stiff and straight before him. 'You going to drop 'em?'

'If I have to.' It was a lament.

'I have no other way of knowing, son, until I take a look and, believe me, if there were I would. This is going to be as much fun for you as it is for me, but I need to find out what's causing your bleeding.'

The cowboy stood up, uncurling like a snake that had just found some winter sun.

'So what are you using to mop up the blood? Cotton?'

The surprise on the cowboy's face had been replaced by resignation. 'I put a wad of it down there.' He shifted his weight from one foot to the other. 'It gets uncomfortable sometimes.'

'How long have you been bleeding?'

'Started a couple of months back, not a lot at first but getting more now. Can itch like hell too.'

The cowboy didn't get to see the concern on the physician's face. 'Two months?'

'Yes sir.'

'How old are you?'

'Twenty-three. Twenty-four the month after next.'

'Mmmm.' The noise came from deep in the doctor's throat and sounded like a growl.

The cowboy looked at the older man, enquiring. 'What?'

'Normally only occurs in a man twice your age or more. You lost any weight?'

'A bit.'

The doctor looked at the young man's leather belt that now hung open. 'Have you pulled it in a notch or two?'

'Three.'

'How many stone have you lost in the last two months?'

'One. Maybe two, but I've been on a drive up from Waco. Always lose some weight on a drive.'

'Eating?'

'Sure. I eat whatever is put in front of me.' The belt-buckle made a clunk on the floor as the trousers fell.

'Mmmm.'

'What?' asked the cowboy, now concerned with the noises the doctor was making.

'I just said mmmm.'

'It didn't sound good.'

'Mmmm?'

The cowboy started to reach back down towards his crumpled britches. 'I'm going.'

The doctor saw a bony wrist protrude from the dirty cuff of

his shirt. 'You're not well, son, and you and I know it. You've known it for two months while I've known it for less than two minutes. But I'm here to help as best I can, so you turn around and bend over and let me take a look, then we can figure out what to do.'

'You're not going to stick anything up there, are you?'

'Not if I can help it. But I need to see first.'

The cowboy turned around in small shuffling steps then lifted his shirttail as the doctor unbuttoned the trapdoor of the young man's long johns.

'Bend over and part your cheeks for me.'

The physician could see a mass of bloodstained cotton waste packed in tight between the cowboy's legs. He took a pair of metal tongs and started to tug at the wad, pulling away fibrous clumps stained black with congealed blood. Then carefully he placed the mire into a yellow enamel bowl.

The cowboy let out a yelp at each yank; the inside of his legs were streaked with dried blood.

The doc leant across towards the washstand. 'I'm going to have to clean you up so I can take a good look. How often do you change this?'

'Every couple of days.' The answer came out part whisper and part whimper.

'You a little worried?' asked the doctor.

The young man nodded in silence, his eyes squeezed shut.

'I can understand that, but this is more common than you think. It's just we don't like to talk about it, because, well, it's personal. Getting shot or cut is different, bit like a badge of honour, but bleeding from the. . . .' He didn't finish.

The young man nodded again, his eyes now open.

The doctor started to wipe away the dried blood with a moist cloth. The room was now silent except for the sound of water being squeezed from the rag after each renewed dunking in the washbasin. Then the doctor said, 'Damn.'

'What is it, Doc?'

'I was hoping like hell you had haemorrhoids from spending too much time in the saddle, but you've got nothing protruding, nothing at all. You're just leaking.'

'What does that mean?'

'Means. . . .' The doctor drew in a breath, then looked down into the basin at the red water. 'It means I can't fix it.'

'Why not? Can't you give me a medicine? A potion?'

'No. There's no potion for what you've got. It's all on the inside, a growth within you, in the gut, somewhere.'

'What does that mean?' Ford asked again.

The doctor continued with the clean-up in silence.

'Doc?'

The physician looked grim. 'You want it straight?'

'Sure I want it straight. That's why I've come to see you.'

'Well, it means you'll make your twenty-fourth birthday but probably not your twenty-fifth. What you've got isn't good. I can give you something better to mop up the blood and some ointment to deal with the itching, but I can't fix this. No one can.'

'What should I do?' Ford's voice showed his bewilderment.

'You don't belong to this town, do you?'

'No. I'm from Round Rock.'

'Texas, eh?' said the doctor.

The cowboy nodded. 'Got here three days ago and was paid off with the rest of the team. They have now headed back south, left this morning.'

'Then follow them up. Go back home to your family in Texas and make yourself comfortable.'

'Got nothing back there, not any more. I had planned to head north for a bit, to try my luck in some place new.'

The doctor wiped away the last of the dried blood from the inside of the cowboy's legs. 'You've been paid, you said?'

'Three months' wages.'

'Well then, go spend a little of it on yourself. Maybe some wine, women and song. It's all here in Sedalia.'

'I guess I could do with a drink.'

9

'Expect you could. Let me get you some padding.' The doctor left the small room, then returned holding an oblong white pad. 'I think you'll find that this will work better. More comfortable and it can take a lot more blood.'

'What is it?' The cowboy took it from the doctor and began to examine it closely, his pants still down around his boots.

'It's. . . .' The doc screwed up his nose a little, then looked away. 'It's a cotton cloth menstrual pad; it's not unlike the pads I used for gunshot wounds during the war, but I can't deny what it is, it's a woman's menstrual napkin. You can wash it out and I'll give you some to take with you.'

The cowboy looked up at the doctor, his eyes glassy and his lip quivering ever so slightly. 'Doc, will I need to wear one of these all the time?' Then he added. 'Till I go?'

'I'm afraid so.' The physician's head dropped a little. 'Nothing else I can offer. I'm sorry, son.' The older man put his hand on the young cowboy's shoulder in the gesture of a father. 'I wish it were otherwise.'

'Nothing else? You can't do nothing else?'

'No, I'm afraid not. I have nothing left to offer you.'

The cowboy positioned the pad between his legs, then drew up his trousers. 'If you have nothing left on offer, then that leaves me with no future, no nothing, doesn't it?'

Doctor Kelvin Peck didn't answer.

Ford's hands pulled on the belt-buckle. 'I guess if there is nothing' – he pushed the leather tail through the large loops on his pants – 'then I have nothing left.' He tucked the tail of the belt away before he looked up. 'Nothing left to lose, have I, Doc?'

The doctor thought for a moment or two. 'No I guess not,' he said in a tone of resignation. 'Nothing left to lose.'

2

ONE ROSE LEFT

Jacob Hicks was the lone barman in the Arcadia saloon that night, as he carefully polished the whiskey glasses, and watched the half dozen patrons. The cowboy at the far end of bar was also on his own, his lean frame hunched forward with a foot perched upon the brass rail. He seemed to be deep in thought.

OK, thought Jacob, he's been no trouble since he walked in just before sundown, but the bottle of Four Roses bourbon whiskey was now three parts empty and his half-closed eyes, along with a hanging head, showed that he was drunk. Very drunk. Maybe he'd make it to closing time, then he'd stagger off back to his boarding house and to bed. Jacob sure hoped so, he hated drunks, especially young drunks who spelt trouble; and he was sick of trouble. He was too old, too tired and his stomach was dyspeptic, again.

'Trouble,' he said, the word coming out as a grunt of displeasure as he placed the glass on the shelf, then threw the well-worn cloth over his left shoulder. He walked slowly down towards the end of the bar and gave a false smile just before he spoke. 'Only got about one rose left,' he said, to open the conversation.

Ford looked up, his eyes glazed and a little confused. 'What?' The cowboy's voice was husky and soft.

The barman's eyes glanced at the bottle with its floral label of four roses in full bloom. 'You've drunk three of the roses.'

The cowboy still seemed confused, then he looked down at the bottle. 'Oh, yeah,' he said slowly, then wiped his sleeve across his eyes.

11

The light caught the cowboy's face and the sight of it took the barman by surprise. Jacob could see that the young man had been crying, so he stepped in a little closer and pulled the towel from his shoulder to wipe the bar. He'd seen crying drunks before but this one was different. He had the look of a mourner who had come straight from the graveside. 'You OK, son?'

The cowboy looked up quickly as if responding to a command. 'Not really,' he said; he wiped his face with the other sleeve, then sniffed.

'Bad news?' the barman asked.

'Yeah, sort of.'

'You know this won't help.' The barman's hand crept towards the bottle then twisted it half a turn.

The cowboy looked down. 'No, I guess not.'

The response was not what the barman had expected. 'They say a man should never drink on his own,' he said.

The cowboy nodded in agreement. 'I don't normally touch the stuff, but I just needed to. . . .'

Jacob Hicks kept his hand on the bottle, then gently started to slide it towards him. 'You don't have to drink it all. You want, I can take it away.'

The cowboy was silent.

'You only pay for what you drank. Might save you some money,' Jacob added.

The cowboy sniffed again. 'Yeah, I've had enough.' Ford's foot slipped off the bar rail as he stepped back, swaying a little.

'Woah there,' said the barman.

Ford grabbed the edge of the bar to steady himself, then he straightened up, slowly sliding the fingers of his right hand into his top left shirt pocket, to pull out a folded wad of greenbacks along with some single crumpled notes. One scrunched note fell upon the bar, unseen by the cowboy, as he examined the money in his hand.

Jacob leant over and took the crumpled note. 'This one will

do fine,' he said.

Ford looked down. 'Where did that come from?'

'Fell from you pocket. You need to be careful.'

The cowboy nodded and stuffed the money back into his top pocket. 'I do,' he said with emphasis. 'This is all I got in this world and might be until the day' – he roughly patted his pocket – 'the day I die.'

'I hope not,' said the barman.

'Me too,' said Ford. The cowboy drew in a deep breath as he stood tall to announce: 'I'm from Texas.'

'I guessed that,' said Jacob.

'Round Rock, Texas.' It was said with pride.

'Round Rock eh? Heading back soon?'

Ford nodded and took in another deep breath that seemed to make him sway a little more, like a slim tree in a stiff breeze. 'It is time for me to say good night, sir,' he said and turned, a little unsteady, swaying on the spot again before he stepped off towards the door.

'Good night, cowboy,' said the barman as he watched Ford Tate's deliberate steps.

Ford returned a lazy wave and the slightest of smiles came to Jacob's lips as he lifted the whiskey bottle, then wiped the bar. So, he thought, the kid wasn't trouble after all, as the rattle of coins upon the bar interrupted the barman's contemplation. Two young men were paying up as the larger one of the two, unkempt and with a dark growth of beard, was leaning in close to whisper a message to his companion. Jacob couldn't hear what was being said, but he knew the other young man was being urged to drink up so that they could both leave quickly.

The barman moved fast, walking back along the length of the bar to press the palm of hand down upon the coins, so that none could be reclaimed before the two men departed. He then quickly counted the cash. The money was correct and he relaxed a little; they weren't trying to run off without paying the full amount. But as he watched the two leave an uneasy feeling in his dyspeptic stomach stabbed sharply against his wide girth. They weren't just leaving – they were following after the man who had just left: the polite but drunk young cowboy from Round Rock, Texas.

3

TEXAS TRASH

The cool night air hit Ford like a splash of autumn creek water as he stepped down from the saloon veranda and on to the dirt street. He drew in a breath, which made him hiccup, so he stopped and took a second deep breath. That started to make his head spin, slowly, tilting the view of the barbershop on the other side of the road. He reached back, feeling for one of the porch posts to brace himself, while he fixed his gaze on the red-and-white striped barber's pole. That too now started to spiral oddly. He closed his eyes for a second or two, then opened just the right eye. The pole had stopped turning, so he started walking, carefully, in halting steps that seemed to jar his spine as each heel scuffed the dirt. 'Homeward bound, Ollie,' he said aloud. 'Homeward. . . .' He opened the other eye and the barber's pole began to turn again, so he placed his left hand over the left eye and continued on his way.

He was close to the end of the street before he realized that he was going in the wrong direction. 'Not homeward bound,' he mumbled. 'Need to turn this steer around and mosey back, Ollie boy. But' – he looked around – 'first things first.' He hiccuped again. 'I need a pee and I need a pee fast.'

To his left an alleyway stretched deep into the dark, down besides Bothwell's Hardware. Towards the end was a docking ramp where an empty buckboard sat. It was positioned close to the wall, its tail hard against the ramp and its two long straight hitching shafts pushed back, so that the poles reached high into the air like horns. Ford caught sight of the silhouette and let out a little whoop. 'Hold fast, dogie,' he said to the wagon, 'while I pee on your leg.' He gripped at the wagon wheel with his right hand and pulled at his belt. 'You better hurry, Ollie-boy, or we're going to have an accident.' His belt came free and his pants dropped to the ground from his narrow hips as he continued to fumble with the buttons on his long johns. When he was free and able to relieve himself, a sense of calm came over him; he closed his eyes and started to hum, swaying slightly, back and forth.

The blow that struck Olford Tate came in an instant – fast, hard and brutal. The clenched fist was aimed at the cowboy's temple but inaccuracy landed it just below the ear knocking him hard against the wagon wheel. His arm passed between the spokes, his shoulder striking the top of the wheel as he twisted and fell, pinning his right arm as he dropped to the ground.

The second blow was also inaccurate. It had been aimed at the centre of his face but as he fell he was saved from its impact. The fist grazed his forehead, then struck the top of his shoulder, wedging his arm down against the hub of the wheel. Instinctively he raised his left arm to protect his face as the third blow struck his hand, forcing it to whack back against his face.

'Get the money,' came the voice from the dark. 'He's down. Just get the money.'

Olford slumped to the ground on his knees but his arm, pinned by the wheel, kept his torso upright.

'Not yet,' came the second voice. 'I want some sport with this Texan, 'cos I hate Texans.'

The blow that followed hit like a thunderbolt. It came from the boot, a kick that struck the side of the cowboy's face on the upper cheek, just below the left eye. It cut like a knife, splitting

15

the skin open so that a squirt of warm blood gushed from the wound, then ran down his neck. The second and third kicks made contact around the body while the fourth struck between his legs and into his unprotected groin.

The battering made the Texan feel as if he was being tumbled down a hill in a water tank, before a sense of lightness, of floating came upon him, as if in one of those odd dreams where the mind seems to leave the body. It was not an unpleasant feeling, just a curious one. Is this death, he wondered?

'That's enough, Zac. Just get the money and let's go.'

'Texas trash,' came the reply. 'That's all he is, Texas trash.'

'For God's sake, Zac, let him be or you'll kill him.'

'No matter, he's just a Texan.'

A hand pulled at Ford's shirt pocket, ripping the corner as the folded money fell at the cowboy's knees.

'Get it all,' called the voice.

The battered cowboy couldn't see who was talking, only that the voice seemed far away in the distance. Then, whack, into his left side came the final blow from a boot that knocked the wind from his lungs. He immediately pulled his arm into his side, trapping his assailant's foot for just a second as he cast his eyes down to see a bright flash. It was at the tip of the boot, a polished metal toecap, embossed, silver, new and smeared with blood.

'Zac, let's go.'

Ford saw the two dark figures standing above him and heard the final words of abuse from the larger of the two men. 'Texas trash.'

'Zachary,' said the other, 'I said let's go, now, he's done for. Let him be, before you kill him.'

4

OUT OF LUCK

The buckboard was halfway loaded when old man Bothwell shuffled from out of the large stockroom at the back of the hardware and on to the landing. In his hand he held a small sack of one-inch nails, weighed, labelled and addressed to the Circle T. When he stepped up on to the buckboard he paused, in some uncertainty, then looked around for a suitable place to stow the goods. He decided to put them up near to the driver's seat. It was then that he caught a glimpse of the Texas cowboy's body, curled up under the front axle next to the wheel that was closest to the wall. He thought at first that it might have been a cloth sack, some debris, discarded during the night.

'Kids,' he said with scorn. 'Damn kids.' But he cut his contempt short when he saw the dark stains of blood on the clothing and upon the ground. He climbed forward over the cargo, carefully, like a frail long legged spider, on to the driver's seat, then down to the ground. He leaned in underneath the buckboard to take a closer look. 'Oh no,' he mumbled before calling, 'Lindsay. Lindsay, you get on down here. There's a man under our wagon and I think he's dead.'

Lindsay was old man Bothwell's only son and he came immediately to his father's call. 'Where, Dad?'

'Under here.'

Although now in his fifties and a little overweight, Lindsay was a strong man from a working life of lifting and putting. 'Let me in, Dad. Let me see.' He put a hand on either side of his father's shoulders and eased him back out of the way, so that he could bend down and crawl in under the buckboard.

17

The body lay on its side with the face almost turned to the ground. Lindsay put a hand on Ford's shoulder and gave a gentle shake. There was no response, so he shifted a hand towards the head and touched the side of the face. The skin was caked with congealed blood and dirt, but it was warm, just. 'Dad.'

He got no response.

'Dad, you hear me?'

The response was a muffled 'yes?'

'Dad, we've got a hurt man here – real hurt. Go tell Pearl to get on up to Doc Peck's and tell him I'm on my way with a wounded man. You stay and keep an eye on the store. I'm going to ease him out and lift him up on to the landing.'

'Pearl,' called the old man as he shuffled off. Then he stopped. 'You want to wheel him? Be easier. I can get a wheelbarrow from inside.'

'No, he not a heavy one, I'll carry him. Be faster,' said Lindsay Bothwell as he started to pull the injured cowboy back out from under the wagon by sliding him along the ground as gently as he could. 'Oh Lord,' he said as he sighted the young bloodied face with its heavily bruised eyes and deep gash on the left cheek. 'I haven't seen the likes of this since Charles Town, but that was war.'

Doctor Kelvin Peck wiped Ford's face with a wet sponge, the water washing dirty into the enamel bowl.

'I don't know who he is,' said Lindsay.

'I do,' said the doctor. 'His name is Olford Tate and he is from Round Rock, Texas. I got a card for him. Saw him just yesterday. Looks like he's been run over by a herd of buffalo.'

'He's been in a stampede all right,' said Lindsay Bothwell. 'But it wasn't buffalo or cattle that got to him. He's been set upon and I had to hitch his britches up. They were down around his legs.'

'So, Lins, what do you think has happened here?' The

18

doctor didn't look up but kept flushing water over the deep wound on the side of the cowboy's face.

'I'd say he was relieving himself next to our wagon sometime last night and got attacked. He was probably drunk.'

'Yeah, I guess he was, but it's a bit hard to put up a fight with your pants down around your knees.' The doctor turned Ford's head to one side. 'He's also been hit from behind, see here.' He pointed to a mark just behind the ear. 'I don't see a lot of men with injuries from being jumped. Most fights are face to face, so I'd say we have a coward in town, one who is out looking for easy marks.'

Ford's face was almost clean and was showing swollen skin stretched blue with bruising and patchy red welts. But it was the deep gaping gash to his cheek that looked most alarming to Pearl. It seemed to cut deep to the bone, showing white below the bloodied purple flesh.

'Did a knife do that?' she asked.

The doctor looked closely. 'It was something with an edge and delivered with heavy force. If it had struck higher, to the eye, then he would have lost his sight.' Doctor Peck looked up. 'Lins, if you and Pearl can spare me a little time, I'd like you to help me while I stitch up his face. I want to do it before he wakes, so if you stand here, just behind him and hold his head real still, and Pearl, I'd like you to stand over there and hold his hand and tell me if you feel it move.'

The two moved into position without saying a word.

'Before we start though, you want to check his pockets for me, Lins? He told me yesterday that he had just been paid but I suspect he's been robbed.'

Lindsay slid his fingers into the open flaps on the shirt pockets. The left one was torn away. 'These are empty,' he announced. Then he tried the trouser pockets, to retrieve a screwed-up red-and-blue bandanna but nothing else. 'Not a cent on this boy,' he said. 'Seems he's out of luck.'

'Luck?' said the doctor. 'That's one thing this cowboy is way out of. Yesterday he received some bad news and now this happens to him. He is way out of luck.'

5

A SILVER TOECAP

The pale-blue embossed pattern looked familiar but for the life of him, Ford couldn't figure where he had see it before. So he closed his eyes for a moment or two and thought: when, where, in a dream? He opened his eyes and saw the face of Doctor Kelvin Peck leaning in close examining him.

'Doc?'

'Yep, back with me again.' A finger prodded his cheek to jab at his tender face.

'Oowee!' The pain was razor-sharp and seemed to run in a line below his eye and into his ear.

'Did that hurt?' The doctor's voice was matter of fact.

'Yes.' Ford's voice was prickly. He lifted his left hand slowly to his cheek and felt the puffy skin, then the hairlike end of the catgut sutures.

'Thought it might,' said Doc Peck. 'You've been stitched up. I haven't covered the wound; I want it to dry out. It's been cleaned up with iodine, that's what woke you up, but don't touch it and keep it clean. If it gets infected it could be bad. It's a deep wound.'

Ford felt a gentle pressure on his right hand and turned his head to see a woman with a placid smile on her round face. She squeezed his hand again and it felt good, but when he tried to smile back his face hurt.

'Doc?'

'Yes, Olford Tate of Round Rock, Texas.'

'How the hell—' He checked his words. 'Sorry ma'am,' he said slowly.

'You were found outside the hardware store this morning,' said Pearl, as she continued to caress his hand. 'Looks like you were set upon and beaten.'

'Robbed too.' The deep voice behind Ford took him by surprise.

'Robbed?' he repeated. 'My earnings, gone?'

' 'Fraid so,' said the doc. 'You're going to be black, blue and sore for a week or two but no bones seem to be broken. Your cheek was cut open, deep, but I've kept the stitches small and close. You'll sport a mark from now on and if you were a European aristocrat you could tell people it was a fencing scar, although it looked more like a sabre cut when I was cleaning it up.' The doctor's voice seemed somewhat offhand to the wounded cowboy. 'But it won't give you a problem. Might even give you a serious look, like a man of the world, and that's no bad thing for a young cowboy, is it?'

Ford didn't say anything, his head hurt like hell and he was having trouble seeing the pattern on the pressed tin ceiling, so he closed his eyes.

The conversation continued around him.

'Me and Pearl will be heading back, Doc.'

'OK, Lins. I'll send this boy down to thank you two once he is up and about.'

'We may have to help him a little if he hasn't any money,' said Pearl.

Doc Peck nodded silently in agreement while Lindsay Bothwell seemed to ignore her comment.

Ford lay on his back, his eyes closed, his head hurting and trying like hell to remember what had happened to him.

Old man Bothwell looked at the tall, slim cowboy with the swollen bruised face and one eye stained red. Then he leant in

21

close to peer at the neatly stitched wound across the left cheek just below the eye.

Ford pulled his head back a little. 'I believe you found me, sir?'

'I did. Lying under the buckboard all curled up. Thought you was castaways.'

'I came to thank you.'

'Do you know what happened?' The old man's eyes kept examining the wound.

'No sir.'

'Thought not. Been drinking?'

Ford hung his head and said, 'Yes sir.' It sounded more like an apology than an answer.

'We found you with your pants down around your knees. You must have been having a pee.'

The words sparked Ford's memory like a flash-powder burst from a photographer's wand and he could see his hand holding on to the steel tread of the buckboard wheel, as he undid his belt and fumbled to lower his trousers. Then it was gone.

'That's enough, Pa.' It was Pearl.

Ford looked up at the lady with the gentle touch. She smiled. He smiled back and his face hurt.

'We can offer you a little work,' said Pearl. 'Not much, mind, but it will give you some money and you can sleep out back.' She glanced towards the storeroom. 'Only for the week though,' she added. 'Only till you are fully back on your feet.'

The offer was unexpected and a relief. The cowboy stumbled his thanks. 'That's, that's most Christian,' he said. 'Most Christian.'

'Might take more than a week to get over your beating,' said old man Bothwell. 'Bad thing getting licked, but worse getting kicked. You'll be sore for a couple of weeks.'

But Ford didn't hear the old man's prediction, all he heard was the word, 'kicked', and the flash powder exploded again in his head. This time he could see a boot lashing out at his face, fast, hard and violent. A black boot, tipped with a polished silver toecap.

⑥

HENRY OWENS

Ford's resolve to seek revenge upon the man who had attacked him came on his last day of employment at Bothwell's Hardware. It was the result of pondering on his misfortune and predicament. He was now a wounded man with little money and no future, which left him with a feeling that was a little like drowning. But this was drowning in the middle of a large shallow lake where his feet were just able to touch the muddy bottom. Death was slow and could even be avoided through gulps of air, but the chances of making it to dry land still seemed impossible.

He worked in the stockroom in silence and in pain from the physical soreness of a battered body and the mental anguish of a tortured mind, constant reminder of the attack. He worked at a slow pace; shifting stock and sweeping the timber floor clean, as his mind raced, swinging widely between anger, torment and self-loathing. Then there were the lonely nights with just his thoughts and small flashes of memory. What resulted was a mire of self-pity and he knew he had to do something about it, if only to gain some self-respect and stop the unexpected fits of panic.

He had told Pearl that he would return to Round Rock in the next day or two. She had pressed some neatly folded bank-notes into his hand, then kissed him on his cheek. It was all he could do to hide his embarrassment and hold back the tears that came from this act of kindness. This small incident was a turning point, as it steeled his determination to at least try and find the man who had stripped him of his dignity. But his conviction had its limits as he told himself that all he could afford was just one day – twenty-four hours, in which to search for the man with the silver toecaps, before he would depart for Texas.

He had paid up the livery account and could sleep with his horses on that last night in Sedalia, then he would have to go. It was a compromise and he knew it because the thought of confronting his attacker came with dread and fear that rolled his stomach over. But it was the money he wanted back, or at least that was what he kept saying over and over in his head: my money – three months' wages. The thoughts on what exactly he should do, once he found his attacker, were therefore pushed aside. That would be decided when they met and only then, he told himself with a sense of relief.

Jacob Hicks wiped the bar and his towel brushed the hand of the man standing on the other side. The barman looked down and saw that a finger, the one between the middle and the small finger was missing from above the centre knuckle. 'Ever give you trouble?' he asked, glancing up then back down at the hand.

The man turned his hand palm up and began to flex the fingers, the stump jerking about in the air, as he looked down at the missing finger. 'Only when I pick my nose,' he said and laughed out loud.

Jacob didn't. 'Had an uncle who lost a finger, caught in a wet rope that near on pulled it off while unhitching a team from a Murphy wagon. So he cut it off because it was useless. Said it was never going to mend anyway. He used to tell the same joke.'

'Yeah, it's a worn-out joke, I know, I've been telling it for years but the kids still love it.' The man flexed his fingers again and the stump waved.

Jacob turned to leave, but the hand with the missing finger grabbed at his arm, then slowly released its grip. The barman's face was stern but before he could speak, the man leaned in.

'I need a little help. I'm a US marshal.' He lifted his jacket back slowly to show where his badge was pinned, not to his shirt, but on the inside lining of the coat.

Jacob relaxed.

'I'm looking for a man by the name of Zachary Hayes. Have you seen or heard of him?'

'Hayes? No,' said Jacob, shaking his head. 'Is he a local?'

'No, he's from Camden, Arkansas.'

'What's he look like?'

'Strongly built, dark hair that's a little long and untidy, and as confident as hell.'

Jacob shrugged. 'That describes half of my patrons on a Saturday night who stay to closing time.'

'This one has been involved in a killing. Serious killing. A federal judge over in North Carolina.'

Jacob's mouth pulled down at the edges with concern. 'He killed a judge?'

'His father did, but he was there with the rest of the family when he did it. I've got warrants for the lot of 'em.'

'What sort of family is that?'

'The Hayes family, and a bigger bunch of vipers you'd never find. Even a rattlesnake would think twice before sinking its fangs into a Hayes, in case he got poisoned. The father calls himself The Preacher and goes by the name of Elijah, but he's no more a preacher than you or I.' The marshal leant in a little closer. 'He had a dispute with the law over a writ the judge had signed to close down a crooked benevolent fund he'd started. He was collecting money from the poor and promising those fools a seat next to the Almighty in the next life. He and his boys went to see the judge at his home to discuss the matter of the writ but Preacher Elijah Hayes had no Christian charity in his heart, only a .45 Colt Shopkeeper in his pocket. Shot the judge when he opened the front door; his grandson was with him, in his pyjama suit. Put all six bullets into the judge's stomach. Took him six days to die, one for each bullet. The kid went stone cold silent after that and couldn't tell us a thing but the judge did. He named Elijah Hayes.'

'But you said you were looking for Zachary Hayes? Where is this preacher?' asked Jacob.

'The preacher has three sons, two are twins by the name of Joshua and Jonah, and both are deficient but as dangerous as hell. The youngest is Zac and he is reckless and trying to follow in his brothers' footsteps. I lost the other three when they split up, but I've stayed on Zac's tail and followed him here to Sedalia.'

'Is this Zac dangerous?' asked Jacob. 'I don't want no trouble.'

'He's only trouble when he's been drinking,' said the marshal. 'This boy needs liquid courage before he's good for fighting. This warrant' – he patted his hand with the missing finger against his jacket – 'is for his capture. Then, I can find out where his kin have gone.'

The bartender looked the marshal up and down carefully. He guessed that he must have been close to fifty, solid, barrel-chested, maybe carrying a little too much weight around the middle, but, with a good three or four inches over six foot, he was able to hide it. His features were lined and his skin leather worn, while his voice was commanding with a southern inflection that came, maybe, from Georgia way. 'And exactly who are you?' Jacob asked.

'Henry Owens.'

'So Marshal Owens, let me get this straight. You want to apprehend a man who was involved in the killing of a federal judge and you want him to tell you where the rest of his family are so you can arrest them too?'

Henry straightened up a little and nodded. 'In a nutshell.'

'What if he doesn't want to be arrested?'

'I'm sure he don't.' The marshal straightened a little more. 'But I don't expect too much trouble. I've arrested over eighty men for serious crimes and this kid is just one more.'

'What if he doesn't want to talk to you after you do arrest him?' asked Jacob.

The big man gave a grin. 'I can be very persuasive.' Then he winked.

Jacob shifted his weight, showing that he was uneasy with the conversation. 'I just don't want any trouble in this bar. I hate trouble.'

'That makes two of us, but I'm going to find him and this looks like a good place to start.'

Jacob was looking worried. 'What makes you think this man is going to come into my saloon?'

'It's Saturday night and if he is in town, then he'll go into every saloon sometime tonight, but I don't aim to chase after him. I'm going to buy a little whiskey, sit on it, over there,' Henry nodded towards the centre of the room, 'and wait.' The marshal pulled on his britches to lift them a little. 'Then when he leaves, I'll apprehend him.'

'When he leaves?'

Henry nodded his head. 'When he leaves.'

'Not on my premises?'

Henry shook his head. 'Not on your premises.'

Jacob seemed to relax a little.

'You got a little whiskey I can have, cheap?' asked the marshal.

Jacob looked back towards the wall with its shelves of glasses and bottles. 'I got a quarter bottle of Four Roses.'

'That will be fine, but could you also extend it on the house? After all, I don't plan on drinking much of it, but I can't sit over there with an empty glass. It will look suspicious.'

Jacob raised his eyes.

Henry leaned in close and spoke softly. 'I'm way out of pocket on this one. The Marshal's Office have given me across to the Justice Department and those pen-pushers in Washington are as tight-fisted as a woman's fingers on her husband's pay packet.'

'What you don't drink, you don't pay for and I'll see you for the first couple of glasses,' said Jacob, but it was said with no enthusiasm.

Marshal Henry Owens smiled, then gave another wink. 'I'm much obliged,' he said. 'A citizen helping the law.'

Jacob muttered the word, 'trouble', his stomach burning with unease as he watched the big man slowly turn and make his way towards a small table in the centre of the crowded room, the bottle and glass swinging in his large hand with the missing finger.

7

CHILL

US Marshal Henry Owens didn't see Zachary Hayes enter the Arcadia saloon. His chosen position, in the centre of the room surrounded by a sea of noisy patrons, might have been good for disguising his presence but it also obscured his view of the main door. However, that wasn't the only weakness in Henry's vigilance. He had just drained the last of the contents of the bottle of Four Roses.

It took Jacob to alert him. The barman came to his table, leant in close and wiped the surface vigorously, as if to remove a stain. 'Over on the back wall, just to the side of the bar,' he said through tight lips. 'May be your man, in a dark shirt, just joined the game and is loaded with cash. He's ill mannered and spoiling too. Not a local and his hair is dark and needs a cut.'

Henry reached out and grasped the bartender's arm so that he couldn't move; then, slowly, he stood to look through the crowd from behind the rotund frame of Jacob. He stared hard across the room towards the gaming tables at the far end of the saloon but three standing customers obscured his view.

Jacob went to move but Henry held his grip, firm and strong. 'Not yet,' he said, his voice low but commanding.

The man standing in the middle of the three, who continued to conceal Henry's line of sight, moved to resume his seat as he bade farewell to the other two men. The view was almost clear but not quite, as the half-stooped figure shook hands and nodded his head in farewell. The time taken with this brief departure could be measured in seconds, but for Jacob this moment seemed to crawl by with the speed of a toothache, while he continued to be held in a vicelike grip. Then at last, Henry could see; his fingers squeezed Jacob's arm and he said, without taking his eyes from his aim, 'It's him.'

Jacob let out a little cough and tasted the dyspeptic bile in his mouth as he felt an icy chill run down the length of his spine. It was trouble, he knew it, he could feel it in his bones, and Jacob hated trouble.

8

JUST FIVE MINUTES

Ford's handgun was a fourteen-year-old Colt Model P. He had purchased it from the owner of a livery stable in Waco, who had taken it in part-payment from a Mexican who had gambled away the last of his money but had then wanted his horse back to return south. It was a gun that had seen better days. The original side plates on the handle had long gone, to be replaced with black walnut grips that had since cracked through lack of a good oiling. The Mexican, or one of the previous owners, had cut a groove in the wood and wrapped a thin wire band around the handle to hold the damaged plates together. The gun worked OK but Ford used it infrequently. If he was going to do any shooting he preferred his Winchester '73 rifle. In fact, the reason he had bought the dilapidated Colt, apart from the cheap price, was because it took .44-40 cartridges, the same as his Winchester. With the Winchester he could shoot straight and far; with his handgun he needed to be up close.

When he acquired the gun it came with a holster, but not one that was made for the Model P. It was an old leather field cavalry pouch made for a long-barrel revolver, so his piece sat low down and snug. Once again, a previous owner had used some poor handiwork to modify the holster by cutting off the original leather flap that once covered and secured a pistol. All in all, this jerry-built set-up worked, but its look and feel showed to all that this was a poor man's rig. As if to accentuate the deficiency of the assembly, Ford wore the gun high on the left hip and forward towards his belt-buckle, to keep it out of the way when he was working. The grip of the pistol also pointed forward and he had to reach across his body to pull it free with his right hand. But this slow and clumsy set-up was of little concern to Olford Tate, as he had never pulled a gun in anger on any man, nor did he intend to. He had had no need. Mr Dennison, the team boss, who had hired him and the other junior hands in Waco, had asked him if he had ever been in a gunfight, before he signed him on. Ford had told him no.

'Good,' said Dennison. 'If we have any disagreements in this team and they can't be resolved by the tongue, then it will be by fists and fists alone. The only time to pull a gun is when you mean to use it, and there's no dispute amongst honest cattlemen that will warrant such action during this drive. You see that, Ford?'

Ford replied in earnest. 'Yes sir. I do, Mr Dennison. I do.'

Earlier that evening, after Ford had washed up, he had taken the old Colt from its big holster, removed the cartridges, wiped them clean, then tested the pistol's action by drawing back the hammer and squeezing the trigger. The hammer, with its pointed firing pin, flicked forward with a sharp metallic click. He then reloaded the handgun with five rounds, leaving the hammer forward and over the sixth empty chamber.

But such serious preparations earlier that evening had now given way to timidity. He was stone cold sober and tired as he searched the saloons, head down, looking for boots with a silver tip.

The bruises on his face had turned a yellow colour like a dirty stain upon a cloth, and the looks he received when he entered each saloon were those of derision. A casual glance could tell that he had come out on the wrong side of a fight.

At the Golden Nugget he'd been jeered by three men of his own age who wanted to know what he'd lost as he looked down at the boots along the bar. They then followed him around the tables, making chicken noises. It brought heckles from the crowd so he left, annoyed at their antics and with himself. At the Star, Ford had been jostled by two older men, who accused him of looking to pick their pockets. His apology was dismissed with anger and the barman told him that he was not welcome.

He was shuffling, hunched forward with his collar up and hands in his pockets, when he passed the Arcadia. He went to walk on, to go back to the livery stables, but he glanced back over his shoulder, then came to a stop.

Five minutes, he told himself. Give it five minutes and then you can say you tried, that you went looking but were unable to find the man who stole three months' wages from your pockets. But he was still undecided as his stomach churned with fear. Then the voice called again from deep within, five minutes, Ollie, just five minutes to find the man who also stole your dignity. Ford turned to face the saloon and the urge to run

31

away gripped and pulled at his legs. 'Five minutes,' he said
aloud. 'Just five minutes.'

9

SO BE IT

The Arcadia was crowded with patrons who all seemed to be
talking at once, their chatter filling Ford's ears as he squeezed
between the bodies, excusing himself as he passed, looking,
searching, for the boots with the silver tips. But before he was
even halfway into the large room he realized that his task was
becoming impossible. Maybe, he told himself, he could wait on
the veranda and watch as the drinkers left. Or maybe he could
just go, give up and head back to Texas.

He rubbed a hand across his forehead and felt the sweat on
his palm, and when he dropped his arm to his side he became
aware of a cowboy looking at him, his eyes wide and staring,
spoiling for a fight. Ford glanced away and turned to leave,
pausing for two men who were deep in conservation and block-
ing his way. Just as they acknowledged his presence and started
to step to one side, he heard a voice shout out loud and sharp
from the back of the room. It just said one word. 'Trash.'

With a flash he recalled the silver-tipped boot striking his
face and the venomous call of 'Texas trash'.

Ford turned but he couldn't see from where the voice had
come. Tentatively he edged in small faltering steps towards the
back wall, past the staring cowboy and towards the crowded
tables. Then he heard it again.

'These cards are trash. I swear all my winnings will be gone
if I keep getting hands like these.'

The man who spoke sat close to the wall, leaning his chair on the rear legs and rocking slightly. Ford looked hard, trying to recall the face. Was this the man? Was this the thief? Was this the one who had assaulted him? He desperately searched his mind but he could recall nothing, except the blow of the boot upon his face.

He stepped a little closer and tried to glance under the table to get a sight of the man's boots, but he was on the far side of the table and could see nothing.

The man laughed as he picked up two cards. 'That's better,' he announced as he casually lifted his foot up on to the edge of the table, to display a polished black boot with a silver tip.

Ford passed his right hand across his body and slowly pulled his Model P from the holster. As the muzzle came free he pushed the handgun under his jacket towards the small of his back, so that it was now obscured from view. Then, with small but deliberate steps, he nudged through the crowd, his eyes fixed on the man with the cards held near his face, until eventually he eased himself in close.

'It's a full table,' said Zachary Hayes to Ford without looking up.

'I'm not here to play cards,' said Ford.

'Then back off,' said Hayes, still looking at his hand.

Ford didn't move.

Hayes looked up, his face showing immediate surprise as he recognized the man he had attacked.

'I'm here to get the money back you stole from me,' said Olford Tate.

'What are talking about,' replied Hayes, but his voice betrayed his unease.

'You stole from me three months' wages, less what I had spent on boarding and liquor. Mr Dennison paid me forty dollars a month plus a bonus of thirty-five. One hundred and fifty-five dollars in all. I reckon you made off with one hundred and thirty. Now I want it back, then I will leave.'

Hayes gave a nervous laugh. 'I ain't giving you any money. Not to you or any other piece of Texas trash who comes making up stories.'

Two younger men at the table laughed. It seemed to give Hayes confidence as he smiled a little and leant back, rocking in his chair.

'I'm not making up stories. It's just the money I want, nothing else. You beat me up bad from behind, but that was my fault for not being on my guard. Give me one hundred and thirty dollars and I will leave you be.'

Hayes was now aware that all surrounding eyes were upon him as he shook his head. 'No. Not now, not never. You'll have to kill me first before I will give you one liberty dime from my pocket.' His words were addressed to the nearby crowd, not to Ford.

Ford stepped forward, pulling the Colt from under his jacket. He thrust his arm forward, the end of the barrel connecting with Hayes's forehead to push his head back hard against the wall, as his foot dropped from the table to thump upon the floor.

The saloon fell silent; all eyes were now fixed on the table at the end of the room. Ford continued to press the muzzle of his revolver against Hayes's head. 'I only want what you took, no more.'

Zachary Hayes was trapped and nervy but he mustered all the bravado he could. 'You don't have the bottle,' he said as his unseen hand, below the table, edged towards his holstered Smith & Wesson.

'I have nothing left to lose but my nerve, and I don't believe it has deserted me yet,' said Ford. His thumb pulled back on the hammer, rotating the cylinder until a .44-40 cartridge was in line with the barrel and ready to fire.

Zac's eyes flicked ever so slightly as his hidden hand slowly gripped the handle of his gun. 'Prove it,' he said, his voice now at a slightly higher pitch. 'Because I will give you nothing.'

Ford remained still, as if frozen, but in his mind's eye he was reliving every kick – the strike of the silver toecap against body and face, and the pain of the cut upon his cheek – while the concealed hand of Zachary Hayes now started to pull his heavy pistol from its holster.

'Texas trash.' The scorn came with renewed confidence and half a grin.

'Will you give me back my money?' said Ford.

'No,' said Zachary Hayes. 'Not now, not never.' But this bold defiance was said without any understanding of the dangerous state of mind of the man before him.

Olford drew in a deep breath that swelled his chest and a feeling of complete calm swept over him. He knew he had nothing left to lose, but he also knew what he had to gain. He had found and confronted the man who had beaten and robbed him. He had delivered his ultimatum and given him his chance, only to be publicly rebuked. He had come for his money but now there was a far more important prize at stake – his dignity. The slightest of smiles now crossed Ford's lips. 'Well,' he said. 'So be it.'

Zac showed both surprise and puzzlement upon hearing these words, but it was too late for any such contemplation, as Ford's finger was now squeezing the trigger of his Colt Peacemaker.

10

STAY EXACTLY WHERE YOU ARE

The hammer of the Colt punched forward and struck the cartridge, exploding the black powder as if it were a giant mallet upon a massive tin drum. The sound was deafening within the confines of the saloon, and all froze as if time had stopped, their heads now turned as one in the direction of the gunshot. Blue smoke filled the air directly above the table and shafts of light from the lamp upon the wall seemed to cast a fearful glow upon the scene.

But Zachary Hayes, in his twenty-fifth year heard and saw none of this. The spinning .44-40 calibre bullet had instantly and brutally punched a hole in his forehead, sliced through the brain and shattered the back of the skull as it emerged from his head. All in an instantaneous and irreversible flash of a second that in its passing had taken with it a life.

Absolute silence followed the booming noise: a quiet still-ness where once the sounds of drinking and conversing men had prevailed. It was a frozen calm, a hush upon the sea of stunned faces as they looked towards the lone standing figure of the lean cowboy with the smoking gun. The body of his victim sat slumped in the chair, his head forward with the chin resting on his chest and a neat round wound above the bridge of his nose, circled by a dark powder burn. Zachary Hayes's eyes remained open and gazed with a far-away stare upon the table, while the fingers of his left hand, which rested in his lap, palm up, twitched in little spasms and flicks as if ready to roll a dice in a game of chance.

Directly above the deceased's head was a splash of red in an almost beautiful pattern, except for the splintered timber frag-ments where the heavy lead bullet had smashed into the wood panelling.

The saloon remained mesmerized and in a total hush, until the noise of a lone chair scraping its legs across the bare timber floor announced the presence of one who was game enough to stir.

'Everyone stay exactly where you are.' The voice was strong and commanding and came from the centre of the room as the big man slowly stood, his gun holstered but with his right hand upon its grip. 'My name is Henry Owens. I'm a US marshal and I have in my jacket the papers for the indictment of the man who has just been shot dead. His name is Zachary Hayes and he is' – the Marshal paused – 'he *was*, wanted for questioning in connection with the murder of a federal court judge in Asheville, North Carolina. I have chased this no-good low-life through the Smoky Mountains of Tennessee and here to Missouri. I was about to arrest him but I can't do that now. Where he's gone even the good Lord can't reach him.' The marshal now started to move towards Ford, slowly picking his way through the seated patrons who remained unmoved.

Ford stood still, a thin blue wisp of smoke curling from around the chamber of his gun, which remained clenched in his hand. He, like all those around him, could not take his eyes from the slumped body of Hayes.

'Now, son.' The marshal was directing his words towards Ford. 'We are going to walk out of here and down the street to the sheriff's office, so that you can explain to him what led you to kill this fugitive. You got that?'

Ford remained fixed to the spot, looking down at the twitching arm of the dead man.

'Son?'

No one in the room moved.

'Son?'

Ford lifted his head. 'My name is Olford.'

The marshal thought he said Auford. 'OK Auford. Now are you OK with that?'

'Not Auford,' said Ford. 'It's Ol-ford but I prefer Ford.'

'Ford,' said the marshal slowly. 'Right. I got it. Now, are you all right with what we have to do, Ford?'

Ford sucked in a small breath. 'Yes, sir,' he said, his voice clear and calm.

'Good. Now I want you to keep your gun in your hand but down by your side and we will leave together. And,' the marshal now lifted his voice and spoke to all in the saloon, 'I don't want anyone going silly on me and thinking they need to get involved. If I pull my gun from this holster, I will use it. And while I may not be as fast as I once was I'm still pretty handy. And Ford.'

Ford turned his head towards the marshal. 'Yes sir?' His voice was soft and compliant.

'You have my permission to shoot anyone who tries to shoot you on the way out.'

'Yes sir,' said Ford his voice still calm.

'Barman?' called the marshal, his voice carrying towards the bar.

'Yes, Marshal,' came the immediate call from Jacob Hicks.

'You got a shotgun under that there?'

'I have.'

'I would like you to ensure that no one touches or moves Hayes's body until I return with the sheriff. Can you do that for me?'

'I can, Marshal.'

'Good.'

'OK, Ford, it's time to go and see the sheriff, so turn slowly and face me, keep your gun pointed towards the floor and start walking towards the door, I will follow you out nice and close.' The marshal raised his voice to address the crowd who were now starting to murmur. 'So nobody move or get foolish and we will be on our way. OK?'

The murmuring continued.

'OK?' he shouted.

Silence returned to the room.

'OK?' he said again, forcefully.

A sea of heads nodded to a mumbled yes.

'I'll call if I see any trouble on your way out Marshal,' called Jacob, his Remington double-barrel 10-gauge now held above the bar and angled across the barman's rotund chest.

'I'm much obliged for that. Now, nice and easy, Ford. It's time for you and me to visit the sheriff.'

11

DEAD OR ALIVE

'Dead, dead?' asked the Sedalia sheriff of Marshal Henry Owens. 'In the saloon?'

'Yep,' said Henry. 'In an instant.'

'Just one shot?'

'Just the one,' repeated the marshal.

'So this boy is quick?' The sheriff looked across at Ford and showed his surprise as he spoke.

'Not exactly.' The marshal ran the palm of his hand, the one with the missing finger, over the back of his head, smoothing down the hair on his neck. 'But if you can get two of your boys over to the saloon, real quick, to make sure that the body isn't touched, then I can tell you about the deceased while we stroll over and' – Henry nodded towards Ford – 'and Olford here can tell you what he's gone and done.'

'Olford?' said the sheriff, raising an eyebrow.

The marshal ignored the question, continuing: 'And why he's gone and done it. Which will be of real interest to me, too.'

'Brandon, Billy,' called the sheriff over his shoulder to the two young deputies who were standing at the back of the office, straining to hear the conservation. 'We've got a body going cold over at the Arcadia. I want you to get over there fast and clear all the geese back at least ten paces. They can gawk all they want but don't let anybody touch anything. And,' he now looked at his two deputy sheriffs, 'that includes you boys. This US marshal here has papers on the departed, so the federals have a vested interest in this one as well, and I don't want any extra paperwork just because we got in the way of their proceedings.'

39

The two deputies grabbed their hats and made for the door in a rush.

As the door slammed the sheriff said, 'Ol-ford, is it?'

'Yes sir,' said the cowboy. 'Olford Tate but I prefer Ford.'

'OK.' The old sheriff nodded, his large grey moustache moving as he twisted his face a little. 'When we get down to saloon I'm going to get you to show me, and I mean *show* me, cos I'm going to get you to walk it through and tell me at the same time exactly what you did. And all I want is the plain truth, no trappings, we'll leave that to the newspapers and the magazines. Now I'm not going to clear out the saloon because I want witnesses to come forward to either support or rebut your story. If you tell me how it happened, and those who saw it say it was so, then that part will be done and out of the way. OK?'

Ford nodded.

'But first things first. You need to tell me why you did what you did?'

Ford drew in a breath. 'He robbed me of my wages and wouldn't give them back. I asked but he wouldn't.'

'OK. How did he rob you?'

'Jumped me while I was relieving myself. I had my pants down around my knees.'

'That sounds like Zachary Hayes,' said Henry. 'He was not known as one who liked to fight fair.'

'How much money?' asked the sheriff.

'Three months' wages and my bonus, less what I spent. I reckon one hundred and thirty dollars.'

'So you killed a man for one hundred and thirty dollars?'

'He said I would have to kill him for it,' said Ford. 'So I did.'

'I see. I think it might be best if I take your handgun, for safekeeping.'

'You'll leave this man defenceless, Sheriff?' said Henry. 'Hayes may well have companions with him who will come looking for young Ford here.'

40

Ford undid his buckle and began to slide the looped holster from the belt. 'He did have someone with him when I was jumped but I have no argument with him. It was just the one with the silver toecaps who gave me the thrashing and robbed me, so you can have my gun.'

The sheriff took the holster, withdrew the Model P and inspected it. 'You can have it back in the next day or two, but why I can't imagine. Looks like it's been used as a doorjamb in a whorehouse. You rough on all your guns like this?' he asked.

'It was how I bought it. I don't use it much. Prefer my rifle,' said Ford.

'He can't carry a rifle around town to protect himself,' protested Henry.

'No he can't,' said the sheriff, exerting his authority. 'So you federals will have to look after him until I inspect the weapon that killed this man Hayes.' His tone had more than a touch of condescension.

Henry didn't respond.

The sheriff placed Ford's Colt on his desk then pinched a thumb and forefinger across the end of his moustache, which seemed to pull his head towards the marshal. 'Now, you said you've got papers on this dead man, so, how were you planning to take him, dead or alive?'

'I wanted him alive.'

The sheriff frowned and pulled again at the end of his whiskers.

'But,' continued Marshal Henry Owens, 'the warrant covers him dead or alive. He's got a one-thousand-dollar reward on his head.'

The look on the sheriff's face slowly turned from concern to relief, then the corners of his moustache started to turn up as he smiled widely. 'Well, don't that make the paperwork easy, real easy,' he said, 'and Ol-ford. . . .' He looked at the young man.

The cowboy looked back, his face impassive, 'I prefer to be called Ford.'

'Ford,' corrected the sheriff. 'Seems you are going to get all your money back and more.'

12

A REPUTATION

'Now you and I need to talk, Ford.' Marshal Owens drew the name out, long, while leaning in close as they walked out of the saloon. He then put his arm around the cowboy's shoulder.

Ford felt a little uneasy but deferred to the marshal's position and authority. 'Now?' he asked.

'Now,' repeated Henry. 'You may have made the sheriff's life a lot easier by not giving him any paperwork but you've made mine a lot harder. I needed to speak to Zachary Hayes. I needed him to tell me where his kin went, but you have just cactused that. The only person he's talking to right now is breathing fire.'

'He might not have been very talkative to you,' said Ford naïvely.

'Oh yeah?' said the marshal. 'Well, you don't know how good I am at persuading people in my custody to converse with me. But Hayes is not my immediate problem.'

Ford felt the marshal's hand squeeze his shoulder.

'You and me were facing the same inconvenience less than an hour ago.'

Ford waited for the marshal to continue, but he didn't.

'Marshal?' he asked.

'Ford.' Henry drew the name out once again. 'I'm out of pocket.'

Ford still didn't seem to understand what the marshal was

alluding to.

'I'm close to broke,' said Henry.

Ford now seemed to understand and nodded his head. 'Do you need a loan?'

'Noooo, I don't need a loan, Ford. Damn it. That was my scalp you're about to put in your wallet. All one thousand dollars of it.'

Ford now got it. 'Oh,' he said. 'Were you looking forward to collecting that reward?'

'You bet I was, and I had no plans of sharing it.'

'Oh,' said Ford again, genuinely concerned.

'Oh,' repeated Henry with a touch of sarcasm.

Ford thought for a moment. 'You can have it,' he said. 'I only want what was taken from me.'

Henry immediately softened his tone. 'No, I don't want it all, but if you were benevolent enough to split it, businesslike, down the middle, then I would be obliged.'

'Five hundred each?'

'Five hundred each, and' – Henry paused – 'and, I'll get you a new gun. Well, near new. I've got a four-and-three-quarter-inch Model P with beautiful balance, better than that five-and-half of yours that looks like it's about to fall apart.'

Ford was surprised at the marshal's generosity. He'd never been given a gift of such magnitude before.

'Took it from a horse thief near Hannibal who lifted it from a railroad guard in Kansas City. It comes with a holster, not fancy but a damn sight better than that leather handbag you've been carrying around on your stomach. This one will sit easy on your hip.'

'That would be real nice,' said Ford. 'And I'd be pleased to share the reward with you, Marshal.' He tried to continue but the words wouldn't come out. He tried again, then stuttered little, 'I . . . I never expected for it to turn out this way. It still feels a lot like a dream. I've never killed a man before.'

'Snake,' said the marshal in reference to the deceased, but

Ford didn't seem to hear.

'I can still see his face. Real clear.'

'That'll never leave you.' Henry had taken his arm from Ford's shoulder and was feeling around in the pockets of his jacket. 'You always remember the first, it never leaves you.' He was now looking for his tobacco. 'You smoke?'

'No sir.'

'You didn't seem to have any trouble pulling the trigger, though?' Henry found the small leather pouch.

'No sir.' The words showed determination. 'I did what I had to do. He wouldn't give me back my money. He gave me no choice.'

Henry was now looking for his cigarette papers.

'I expected for him to kill me before I got to pull the trigger. But he didn't,' said Ford.

'No, but I bet he was close. Could you see his gun hand?'

Ford thought for a moment. 'No sir.'

'Henry. It's Henry.' The marshal stuck the corner of the cigarette paper to his bottom lip. 'You've always got to keep an eye on their gunhand. And watch out for lefties.' Henry was looking down as he spoke, rolling the tobacco in the palm of his hand, the paper on his lip waving gently as he spoke. 'That snake would have been going for his gun, that would have been for sure. But I've got to pay it to you. You stayed cool and did it anyway.'

'Yes. . . .' Ford stopped, as he was about to say 'sir' again. 'Yes, Henry,' he said.

'Mmmm. You are a cool one.' Henry was shaking his head and smiling; then he ran his tongue along the edge of the rolled cigarette.

'But it turned out different, didn't it?'

Henry glanced up at Ford. 'Yes it did, but life can be like that, kind of amusing, sometimes, but only sometimes.' He placed the crushed and twisted cigarette in his mouth. 'So what are you going to do with your money and your reputation?'

'Reputation?' asked Ford.

'Oh, yes, you now have a reputation. You killed a fugitive, a wanted man, a man with a price on his head. The papers will write about you. The chronicles in the East love to hear about such business, about the lawlessness of the West. Gets them real excited.'

'I was going to head back to Texas, to Round Rock.'

Henry was now searching for a safety match. 'That's where you may be heading, but what are you going to do with the money?'

Ford thought for a little. 'I'm going to buy a gravestone.'

Henry's head jerked back a little. 'And who would that be for?'

Ford thought for a moment. 'My mother. When she died we could afford nothing but a wooden cross, and that was when I was fourteen, nearly ten years ago, it would have been eaten out by the ants long before now. I'd like to give her something more permanent.'

'Your dad not around?'

'He died in '62 at the Battle of Gaines's Mill. It was the year after I was born.'

'And your mother, what did she die of?'

'Scarlet fever.'

'Got any siblings?'

'Only my older sister Celia is left. We were both fostered by the neighbours after my mother passed.'

'Good neighbours.' Henry was nodding his head in approval.

'They were the same ones who burnt down our house. They were worried about the infection from the fever. They said they had to do it. That they had no choice.'

'Mmmm, is that so?' Henry had found a match and its flame flared as it lit the end of the cigarette, which was now squashed in the middle. 'So when do you leave for Round Rock?'

'I was planning to leave tomorrow. I was on my way to turn

in and rest before I left, when I thought that I would take one last look for the man who stole my money. I was feeling tired, but I don't feel tired any more.'

'I expect not,' said Henry. 'Killing a man sort of does that, it gets the mind racing; I saw it during the war. What you need is some preoccupation. You feel like a drink?'

'No,' said Ford, his answer resolute. 'Liquor got me into this trouble.'

'It does that.' Henry brushed off some ash that had fallen on to his arm. 'What about women? What say you and I go to the bathhouse?'

Ford went to say yes but he stopped. He knew he couldn't sit in a warm tub if he was bleeding, no matter how much he'd like to have his back washed by a beautiful dove, so he just said, 'no,' again.

Henry drew back on the cigarette, then looked at it with displeasure. 'That only leaves one thing, son. You want to go to the opera?'

'I've never been to the opera.'

'Well, it will have to be tomorrow night. Tonight we'll lean on the sheriff to let us sleep in one of his cells, save us a little cash so we can spend up big tomorrow. Might also get you some new duds.'

Ford looked down at his dirty baggy trousers.

Henry flicked the unfinished butt from his fingers; it flared in sparks before disappearing in the dark. 'Tomorrow it will be then. We'll go to the opera as a couple of Champagne Charlies with you wearing your new duds and reputation.' He put his arm back around Ford's shoulder and gave his arm a squeeze.

Ford half-smiled and was about to speak, but he fell silent as Henry began to hum the tune 'Sons of Temperance', a song that the young cowboy knew well but which seemed to be an odd selection.

13

YOU ONLY LIVE ONCE

The day had passed in a whirlwind for Ford. He was called upon to sign a statement of the proceeding leading up to and including the killing. This was attached to four witness statements given by patrons of the Arcadia. Ford did not see these statements, but the sheriff advised that all was as it should be, and was in keeping with his version of events in the saloon.

Next came the completion of the application for the collection of the reward for the apprehension of Zachary Hayes dead or alive. This was done with Henry's assistance, in a neat hand, which impressed Ford as he watched the completion of the lengthy document, which was then posted off to Washington. Henry also sent a telegraph to the Justice Department, advising of the death of Zachary Hayes and of the claim for bounty. He also advised of his intention to draw funds on his imprest account for services due. This he announced to Ford with authority, as they walked to the branch of the First National where Henry authorized the drawing of one quarter of the full amount of the reward. He then handed $125 to Ford, counting out each dollar as if presenting him with wages due at the end of a long cattle drive. This, along with the $130 returned to him from the pockets of Zachary Hayes, was more money than Ford had ever owned in his life.

'You won't see the remainder of the reward for ninety days,' said Henry. 'And as I have claimed it in my name, I will have to

47

forward it on to you at Round Rock via the First National. On this one,' he added, 'you will have to trust me.'

Ford immediately nodded in agreement, then added, 'Of course,' believing himself to be more than fortunate to have got his money back from the pockets of a dead man.

The last part of the administration, as the sheriff called it, was a short walk to J.L. Evatt, undertakers where the body of Hayes was on display in an unlined coffin. The sheriff carried Hayes's gun with him in a calico sack, and on arrival had the undertaker's two assistants take the coffin from the trestles and lean it upright against the wall. Ford watched them struggling with the weight and bulk of the task and felt decidedly uneasy with these proceedings. This apprehension was not shared by Henry or by the sheriff, who propped Hayes's pistol against the edge of the dead man's waist belt and placed a cold hand upon the grip.

When the photographer arrived he set up his camera immediately in front of the coffin, then ushered the sheriff, Henry and Ford into position. Ford averted his gaze as he didn't want to look upon the face of the man he had shot, who now looked like a wax figure from a carnival sideshow.

'Ready,' called the photographer, his head under the black hood behind the camera. 'Breathe in, hold, don't move.'

The flash lit up the room and brought a spot before Ford's eyes, as if he had looked directly at the sun. When the sheriff took the gun back from the body of Zachary Hayes to return it to the calico sack, he shook the dead hand in a brief moment of mirth. Henry grinned while Ford had to fight a strong urge to flee. He swallowed and felt the sharp taste of bile catch in his throat, so it was with relief that he stepped back into the sunlight and fresh air as they left the undertaker's.

In the early afternoon three newspapermen in suits arrived to interview Ford. Fortunately, Henry did most of the talking, explaining how the Hayes family were a nest of vipers who had brutally killed a judge then run off. He then spoke in detail of how he had chased after them, tracking Zachary Hayes, a violent and unpredictable man of the lowest morals, right to the very heart of the fair city of Sedalia. Henry held a finger aloft, like a politician, as he made his point on the poor nature of the Hayes family.

From there the story seemed to take on new life, with Henry, now standing before the seated pressmen, explaining how Ford, who had been attacked and robbed by Hayes and a number of accomplices, had confronted Hayes in the Arcadia and demanded his money back. Henry, now using a different voice to quote Hayes, said. 'You will have to shoot me first.' Henry then pulled his gun from the holster and the pressmen ducked as the marshal waved it past their faces and said, 'The snake went for his gun but Ford shot first.' Then he added, pointing to Ford, 'This man will return to Round Rock, Texas, triumphant in the doing of this good deed.'

Ford felt embarrassed as he sat in silence with the man from Harper's sketching his features, which included the cut and stitches upon the side of his face.

At lunch Ford only touched the edges of his plate leaving most of his meal for Henry to finish with relish. The feeling that he was still in a dream persisted, especially when Henry took him shopping for new duds, as he called each item of clothing they were shown by the tailor. When Ford stood at last in his new ensemble to look into the full-length mirror he was astonished at the image that stared back.

'You look dapper,' said Henry, and Mr Pembroke the tailor nodded in agreement.

What Ford saw before him was a man of presence, distinction even, and these were qualities that the young cowboy had never thought he could possess. But it was the events of that evening that were to mark a most important occasion in his short life.

'Madam,' said Henry with authority. 'We are two gentlemen

looking to purchase two seats for tonight's performance by Madam Marie Rosine, preferably in the centre, not too far back.' Henry glanced over towards Ford and winked before turning away to speak to the woman in the small ticket booth.

Ford couldn't hear her reply but he could hear Henry.

'Well, if all the seats are sold, then we will purchase standing room.'

As Ford waited he looked up at the front of the theatre with its large painted banner titled La Trotto Opera Hall. Then he looked down at the thin blue lines in the weave of his trousers, which stretched down to his new boots. He wondered if this was really him in such splendid duds.

'What?' called Henry. 'What? Do you mean tonight's concert is completely sold out. I demand to see the manager.'

Ford was stone-cold sober but Henry had been imbibing and swayed a little before he leant in towards the young woman. 'I'm a US marshal and this is my deputy. He is the man who shot dead that son—' He checked himself. 'That fugitive Zachary Hayes in the Arcadia saloon just yesterday evening.'

The woman seemed impressed but not yet persuaded to find room in the La Trotto, as the Sedalia music hall had been christened for that evening's performance.

'He was interviewed today by gentlemen of the press this very day,' advised Henry. 'You will read about him tomorrow in the edition of *The Democrat* and you will be able to tell all your friends.'

She was faltering.

'A telegraph telling the story has also been sent East. This is a nationwide story,' he announced and swayed a little more.

The woman leant out of her seat to get a good look at Ford, then fluttered her eyelids.

'Deputy,' called Henry to Ford.

Ford looked over his shoulder to see whom Henry was talking to. Henry tossed his head to call Ford over, so the cowboy stepped in close to the booth and bent down to look in.

'Good evening ma'am,' he said.

'This,' said Henry, 'is Deputy Ford Tate who with cool and calm resolution, confronted and shot dead Zachary Hayes, a villain of the lowest order.'

She weakened and made an offer. 'I can sell you two seats, but you will be sharing the first-rate seating with Mr Ludlow and his two daughters. It will cost you five dollars.'

Ford was taken aback. That was the best part of three or four days' wages.

'Each,' she then added.

Henry didn't hesitate. 'We will take them, thank you madam.'

Ford pulled his head out of the cramped window frame and hit his crown on the small awning. 'Henry?' he said. 'That's a lot of money.'

Henry seemed unfazed by Ford's concerns. 'You only live once, my boy.'

When they walked up the narrow carpeted hall towards the best seats in the Sedalia music hall Ford tried to ask Henry why he had called him his deputy, but Henry paid no attention. So in silence, except for the creak of the staircase under each step, they passed through the narrow half doors to join Mr Ludlow and his two daughters.

As the two slim half-doors opened, the magic of the music hall seemed to burst upon them. The first-rate seats were suspended above a sea of people, like a little nest, almost directly above the stage and orchestra pit. In front of Ford, seemingly close enough to touch, was the edge of a deep crimson curtain trimmed with gold that stretched high above them to a ceiling painted with wreaths and flowers. To the left were rows of faces stretching along the curving balcony, smiling, talking and laughing in anticipation. And upon Ford's ears came a cacophony as the orchestra tuned their instruments in preparation for the performance.

'Mr James Ludlow, my daughters, Gertrude and Elizabeth,'

said the dark-suited man who rose to his feet as they entered. He was small of stature but his tone was confident as he turned to introduce his daughters.

'Sir, ladies, Marshal Henry Owens and Deputy Ford Tate,' replied Henry. 'We are pleased to make your acquaintance and join you in this gaiety.' Henry then burped. 'Over here, Ford, you should sit near Elizabeth.'

'Gertrude,' corrected the young woman with the white lace shawl.

Ford manoeuvred carefully within the confines of the box as the lights dimmed, bumping against the young woman as he sat. He apologized. She smiled and he felt his face flush as he silently thanked the fading of the light that hid his bruises and embarrassment.

The maestro's baton struck the stand before him to quieten the crowd as all watched, his arms slowly rising like a bird preparing for flight. Then, just as his hands were at their highest point they suddenly fell and the orchestra erupted as one. A swirling storm of sound rolled over Ford, swamping his senses with an excitement that he had never thought possible, and the audience roared and clapped in appreciation. Ford, now sitting forward on the edge of seat, turned towards Gertrude. 'Wonderful,' he said.

'Yes, wonderful,' she replied, 'but the best is yet to come.'

As the orchestra played the crowd applauded to the parting of the large curtain, which revealed the shimmering figure of a lone woman. She was dressed in a cream, sequinned gown and wore in her hair a large spray of feathers that seemed to sail just above her head. Ford's eyes were fixed upon this wondrous sight as he watched the soprano draw in a deep breath, part her lips and begin to sing an aria from *The Magic Flute* by Wolfgang Amadeus Mozart.

To a hushed silence the assembly of admirers fixed their eyes upon the marvellous sight as the auditorium filled with sharp, clear, perfect notes that soared to the very roof. Each in the audience thought that she was singing just for them, but for Ford, he knew that he was the one, his heart told him so. This angel, this being who had descended from heaven and reminded him of his mother, reached out and touched his very spirit.

Gertrude clasped her hands close to her chin and, like Ford, leant forward to drink in the excitement and the marvel of it all. She turned to speak to the young man next to her, to express her exhilaration, only to notice the glistening tears that streaked down his cheeks. For an instant she was concerned, until she saw the joyous smile upon the young man's face. She turned away not wishing to embarrass him and saw that the marshal had fallen asleep and was starting to snore.

14

THE BAIT

Henry shook Ford's hand with an iron grip. 'You look after yourself and keep that new Model P close at hand.'

'I always prefer to use my Winchester,' replied Ford.

'Keep that at hand too,' said Henry as he kept shaking Ford's hand.

Ford nodded. 'I'll be going, Henry' – he paused – 'and I just wanted to thank you for all that you have done for me.' The cowboy looked at the ground as he spoke and spun his hat in his hands.

Henry looked, a little uncomfortably, skywards. 'No need,' he said. 'Now get out of here and go home, back to Round Rock. I'll telegraph your reward money to the bank when it comes through.'

Ford nodded again, then lifted his new clean boot into the stirrup, pulled himself into the saddle, turned his horse, then gave a self-conscious little wave.

Henry gave a half-wave back.

'I wonder if things will be the same for that boy from now on?' said the sheriff as he watched the departing cowboy.

Henry turned and stepped up on to the veranda of the sheriff's office. 'No, I don't believe they will ever be the same again for Olford Tate.'

'Do you think he'll get into trouble?'

'I sure hope so,' said the marshal.

The sheriff was a little taken back. 'You do?'

'Yep, or how else am I going to find the preacher and his two idiot sons?'

The sheriff looked at Henry, a little confused, then back at the departing figure of Ford who was now halfway down the street. 'You mean?' He thought for a moment. 'You mean you want. . . ?' He stopped again. 'You want that young cowboy to lead you to old man Hayes and his two boys. How?'

'Easy. As soon as old man Hayes reads about Zachary being gunned down in Sedalia he and his boys will go looking for the man who did it.'

'But how will they know where to find him?'

'Ever been to Round Rock?' asked Henry.

'Nope,' said the sheriff.

'Nor me, but I expect it's none too big and easy to find a man by the name of Olford Tate, and that's where those newspapermen have reported he is heading. So. . . .'

The sheriff waited for Henry to finish, but he didn't. 'So, what?'

'So as soon as the preacher reads that, I'll put a year's wage on it he'll be heading to Round Rock.'

'So you set that boy up as bait?' said the sheriff.

'Bait?' said Henry as if studying the word. Then he nodded his head slowly. 'Yes, I suspect I did.'

The sheriff was shaking his head. 'So what do you do now?'

'I follow him all the way to Round Rock.'

'Well, I hope you get there before old man Hayes and his sons do.'

'Well, I don't want to get there too soon, do I? Or I'll spook the—'

'Bait?' said the sheriff.

'I prefer the word "lure",' said Henry.

'You can call it what you like, Marshal, but I'll call it as I see it. And I see it as bait.'

Henry thought for a moment, pushing his lips out, then slowly he nodded his head in agreement. 'Yeah, I guess that's what it is, pure and simple. Bait.'

15

WATCH OUT

Ford had left Sedalia later than he had planned – two days later. Henry had asked if he had ever travelled on his own over such a distance. A distance that required weeks in the saddle.

'Well, that's how I got here,' Ford had replied, not hiding his irritation at such a question.

Henry immediately responded. 'Don't get on your high horse with me, Ford.' He drew the word 'Ford' out long. 'I know you travelled eight hundred miles up from Waco, but that was in a team. You'll be heading back on your ownsome and that's different. You have to be self-contained. Anything goes wrong out there, between settlements, and it's just you, two horses and what you've got left from what you took in the first place.' Henry half-turned, as if ready to walk away. 'I've been doing this caper for twenty years and was willing to give you a hand. But if you don't need it, well then, suit yourself.'

Ford quickly relented and apologized by removing his hat and sucking in a deep breath. 'Your guidance would be most appreciated; thank you, Henry.'

Henry responded immediately by turning back to face Ford. 'Good,' said Henry, 'and I will be only too pleased to provide it.'

Henry in his typical way then took over the proceedings, and Ford had quickly realized that travelling on your own was indeed very different from travelling in a team. He also began to appreciate the extent of the responsibility his team boss, Mr Dennison, had fulfilled in ensuring that all in his team were watered, fed and directed towards their duties.

The preparation for the return journey not only consisted of the selection and purchase of provisions, which seemed to be an endless list, but also the packing of supplies upon his two horses, so that the location of each item was in a place related to its priority of use.

'First and foremost,' said Henry, 'is water. A man can live for a week on nothing but water. I've done it plenty a times. But without water you'll be dead in four days, five if you're unlucky. Dying of thirst is a miserable death. Avoid it if you can.' The words were matter of fact but the consequences were grave and Ford readily accepted the advice.

The provisions also included .45-calibre ammunition for the Model P that Henry had given Ford. This was store-bought ammunition and expensive but, as Ford examined the gleaming gold-coloured cartridges in their cardboard boxes, Henry continued to dispense his wisdom. 'Buy right first and you won't have to buy a second time. You'll get a dozen reloads out of these if you do it right. Will save you money in the long run.'

The last item was a strip map that tracked the route southwest to Joplin, then south to Fort Smith.

'I know Fort Smith well,' said Henry. 'Most US marshals do,

it's where Judge Parker comes from. Good man. We catch 'em and he hangs 'em.' Henry laughed at his own joke but it failed to tickle Ford. 'But this next leg across to the Chisholm Trail,' Henry pointed at the map, 'could be tough. How did you find it on the way up?'

'We had to rely on the creeks. They all had water but most were low,' said Ford.

'Well, I expect they'd be dry by now, so you water up big at Fort Smith, then try to get across to Red River Station without delay. If you see any water top up, but be prepared to see none. Now don't kill your horses doing this leg. How fast were you travelling when your team came north?'

'Ten mile a day, six days a week, rest on Sunday.'

'OK. On two horses you can do twenty-five a day but still stop Sunday and don't just lie around, unpack all your kit and caboodle, lay it out and do any make and mend. Clean both your weapons, too. Take out all the cartridges and oil – lightly, mind you, you don't want sand and grit glued to everything.' Henry pressed his hand against the grip of his own Colt with the carved initials H.O. to emphasize his words.

Ford looked on like a student receiving schooling.

'Now, that routine should get you into Round Rock inside of six weeks and have you and your horses arrive in good order. Of course, once you cross the Red River and are back on the Chisholm you'll be yodelling. Easy ride from there. Might even come across some of your Texas cowboy kin.'

'Expect so,' said Ford as they studied the long map in Doc Peck's waiting room. 'But what about you Henry, where are you going?'

Henry repeated the question back to Ford. 'Where am I going?'

Ford waited, then had to ask again.

Henry didn't look at Ford when he said quietly, 'After the Hayes.'

'Do you want me to go with you?' Ford asked.

57

'Oh, no,' said Henry, looking down at the floor scuffing his boot back and forth. 'No. You head on back to Round Rock.'

'So how are you going to find the Hayes?'

'Oh, well . . . I'll . . . I'll head south. Arkansas, maybe Louisiana.' Then he added with a shrug, 'Even Texas.'

'So we might even get to catch up?' Ford's voice showed renewed enthusiasm.

Henry scuffed the other boot. 'Yeah, we might even get to do that.' He looked up at the tin ceiling. 'I tell you what. If I end up in Texas, I'll come and look you up in Round Rock.'

'I'd like that,' said Ford. 'I'd like that a real lot.'

When Ford stepped from the doctor's room the stitches on his cheek had been removed and, except for the straight thin scar and red in his corner of his left eye, all the other signs and marks on his face were starting to fade. Under Ford's arm was a bulky blue package that he tried, with great difficulty, to hide by shielding it with his hat.

'What's that?' asked Henry.

'Dressings,' said Ford, trying not to be overheard by the other waiting patients.

'What sort of dressings?'

'You know, like in the war, for wounds. Doc said I should take them along with me, in case, for my cut and stuff.'

'Your cut's all but healed.' Henry squinted at Ford's near-healed wound, then back to the package.

Ford added. 'He said, in case I get another wound.'

Henry looked at the bulky pack of tightly wrapped menstrual pads. 'Wound dressing? What sort of wounds?'

'Well, like a gunshot wound,' said Ford in a hushed tone.

'Really,' said Henry out loud as he poked at the package with a finger. 'What are you planning on being shot by, a Gatling gun?'

The final piece of advice from Henry to Ford was, 'And you watch out for rattlesnakes and muleskinners.'

Ford wasn't sure exactly what Henry was alluding to but he

nodded anyway. Maybe Henry should have been more exact, in fact maybe he should have said: 'And you watch out for the Hayes family because now that you have killed one of their kin they will be coming your way to settle the score.' But Henry didn't say that at all. Instead he just made a vague reference to reptiles and mule drivers.

16

RATTLESNAKES AND MULESKINNERS

Henry also left Sedalia later than he had planned: two days later. His intention had been to follow one day behind Ford but a heavy night of whiskey in the company of a woman by the name of Esther at the Row on Howard Street, over near the rail-yards, had left him with a heavy head and a light pocket. And while Henry was good at giving advice, he was less so at taking it, even his own. His preparations had not been as meticulous as those of Ford, so early into his journey he found that he was missing the required quantities of some essential items such dry meat, biscuits, coffee and tobacco, which meant that he would have to restock on the way and pay the higher prices charged by the settlement traders. In addition, he was using up water at a rapid rate, but the creeks were still flowing a little, on this first stage south-west, so he pushed on and asked Lady Luck to cut him a little slack.

At Joplin he was surprise to hear that Ford was now four days ahead of him. The owner of the livery stable, where Ford had had his horses reshoed, waxed on about how well prepared the boy was for his journey to Round Rock. Henry just grunted. If Ford continued at this rate, then Henry would be the best part of a week behind him when he eventually reached his destination. If the preacher and his sons were waiting there for Ford, which Henry expected, then it would be all over before he had arrived.

'All I'll get to see is his grave,' Henry said in a conversation to his horse Shamoose as he pulled himself into the saddle.

'He did say,' said the livery owner, thinking that Henry was talking to him, 'that he planned to have a good break at Fort Smith before heading out to Red River.'

Henry sparked up. 'How long?'

'Not sure exactly, but I think three or four days.'

When Henry arrived at Fort Smith six days later after some hard riding, he learnt that he was now just one day behind Ford. With this news he threw caution to the wind, decided to forgo his stopover and headed off for the Red River Station, across the open country where the Choctaw had been resettled on 250 miles of buffalo grass and sagebrush. But at this time of the year this expanse was devoid of water and teetering on the edge of becoming a dustbowl. It would only come back to life when the annual rains returned and that was not expected for at least another month.

The going was tough over the following week and started to take its toll on Henry. Then, three days out of Red River he hit a low. His water was near out, his horses tired and his spirit frayed. It was at times like these that he felt every one of his forty-nine years and then some. His decision to imbibe was a foolish one but the temptation of the whiskey in his supplies, and his low mood, got the better of him.

When he stirred the next morning the sun was burning upon his face but that was not what had woken him. It was the prod of a gun barrel under his chin.

'He's a waking?' announced the squawking voice with glee. 'Waking from the land of whiskey?'

The other man held the almost empty bottle in his hand. 'Not much left here for us, Seth.'

'He might have more,' said the one holding the gun on Henry.

'No,' mumbled Henry, 'that's all there is.'

'Greedy then, ain't he?' came the reply.

Henry slowly slid his hand down to his holster, his fingers slightly splayed and ready. It was empty.

'Yep,' said the man looking down at Henry's right hand. 'This is your gun, or was. Mine now.'

'Oh no,' said Henry as he forced his eyes wide against the glare of the sun before he looked at the two old men, one crouched next to him, the other standing. 'I've been bush-whacked by muleskinners.'

'We're no muleskinners,' said the one standing, his voice showing annoyance at the allegation.

Henry looked over at the wagon with its three mules side by side. 'Really? You look like muleskinners to me. Now give me back my gun before I get angry.'

'Angry,' laughed the one with Henry's .45. 'If you is angry now, you are really going to be irritated when we finish with you.'

'Oh yeah,' said Henry through cracked lips, his mouth as dry as the river bed he'd camped in. 'And what did you have in mind? Because you'll have to kill me before you take anything from me.'

'Big talk,' said the one standing. 'But we ain't going to kill you. Go killing a man and you end up with a rope around your neck. When we leave we will be able to truthfully say you was alive, but we are going to relieve you of all you own.'

'Everything,' added the kneeling felon with a smile as his free hand pulled on the buckle of Henry's gunbelt. 'Go get the rope, Quint.'

Quint returned with an old rope and the enthusiasm of an irresponsible child.

'Bind him up good with his arms behind his back, then right down to his feet.' Seth chuckled as he gave the commands.

'You boys done this before?' asked Henry, his head hurting like hell.

'Whenever we can. It's far more rewarding than' – he was looking for the right word, then laughed – 'than mule skinning, isn't it, Quint?'

Quint grunted, his tongue protruding over his bottom lip, glistening red and twisting from side to side as he concentrated on the job at hand. He pulled the rope tight around Henry's body, forcing the air from his lungs, then tied a series of looped knots down over his legs.

Henry lay on his side, hogtied, watching as the two old men ratted through his belongs, scattering every item upon the ground before picking them up to throw on to his canvas ground sheet, which they then wrapped and lifted into the back of their wagon. The saddle from his horse Shamoose was taken, as were the pack bags for his second horse Silo. He then saw Seth, the one who had held the gun on him, take the reins of both horses and twist the narrow leather straps around his fist, pulling their heads down as he pointed the Colt .45 between Shamoose's eyes.

'No,' yelled Henry. 'Don't shoot the—' But before he could get all the words from his mouth the gun fired and Shamoose fell sideways kicking sand high into the air. A second shot followed and Silo pitched forward from a bullet that entered the left eye, the head twisting back as he fell, blood running from his nostrils to pool and stain the brown earth.

Henry's face pressed into the ground as he watched the wagon depart to the jingle of dirty black tin pans that hung low from the back of the wagon. He twisted and kicked, trying to get free, but the rope wouldn't budge, so he lay, looking at the two dead horses before he squeezed his eyes tightly shut and cursed himself for his idleness at being caught. And as he cursed he had to fight back the tears of grief and guilt that overwhelmed from a deep sense of shame, and a fear that came from the thought of not being able to get free.

17

BITTEN TWICE

Ford was about two days out of Red River when he saw the wagon heading his way. It was a surprise to see fellow travellers in this desolate place, so he waved his hat as they approached and gave a yell. The two old men waved back, then pulled their wagon in close to look down upon the young cowboy who had laid out his kit and was busy with his make and mend.

'I'm Ford Tate from Round Rock Texas,' he said by way of introduction.

Quint's hand slowly reached down for the muzzle of Henry's rifle, which he had positioned to his right side.

Seth saw the movement and put his hand out to stop him as he called out. 'You heading to Red River?'

'Yes sir. Be there the day after tomorrow. What about yourself?' asked Ford.

'Same place,' said Seth.

'Then where?'

Quint said 'South to—'

But before he could finish he was cut off by Seth who said, 'Here and there,' as he looked down upon the cowboy. 'What are you doing?' he asked as he examined the items laid out neatly on the ground sheet.

63

'Make and mend, resting the horses. I've been making good time but I want to keep them fresh and my kit in good shape.'

'Where did you come from?' asked Seth.

'From Sedalia.'

'You travelling on your own?' Seth looked around as he spoke.

'Yes sir.'

'So you are sort of halfway between nowhere.' The mule-skinner's eyes shifted from the barren skyline back to Ford.

'I guess so,' said Ford, looking around as if he had just noticed for the first time that he was surrounded by nothing but stark landscape.

Seth smiled to show a row of tobacco-blackened teeth. 'Mind if we get down and see what you've got laid out there?'

Ford was starting to feel a little uneasy, and that apprehension heightened when the second old man climbed down from the wagon with a Yellowboy in his hands.

As Seth was poking around Ford's personal items the cowboy did his best to dissuade them by trying to engage them in conversation, but Seth couldn't be dissuaded. 'What's that?' he said looking at the bulky package of menstrual pads.

'Dressings,' said Ford, then he added. 'For wounds.'

'You a medical man?'

'No,' said Ford. He threw the corner of the groundsheet over to cover the parcel, but it fell short. He bent down and pulled at the canvas, and as he did he glanced at the old man's gunbelt and saw the grip of the Colt with the carved initials of H.O. 'What the—' The words had spilt from Ford's lips before he could stop them. He let go of the heavy fabric and moved his hand to his Model P. But it was too late.

'You leave your hand right where it is, son,' said Quint.

Ford turned to see the muzzle of the Winchester pointing directly at him.

'Two in as many days,' said Seth. 'Who'd have thought this dust bowl would be so rich in pickings.'

Quint let out a giggle.

'Get the rope, Quint. We got some hogtying to do.'

As the ropes pulled tight around Ford's body Quint asked of Seth, 'You want me to kill the horses?'

Before Seth could answer Ford started to plead. 'Don't shoot the horses, mister, not my horses. They are good horses and you'll get good work out them. But don't shoot them.'

'We don't need work horses.'

'Then you'll get a good price if you sell them. Everybody is looking for good horses like these.'

Seth shrugged.

'I'll give them to you. I'll sign a bill of sale to say you bought them fair and square, but don't shoot them.'

Seth looked at the horses.

'Please,' added Ford.

'Bill of sale, eh?'

'My word, my signing, saying you bought them from me, fair and square. Once you have that, then you can sell the horses, no questions.'

'Quint, leave one hand free so this boy can sign his horses over to us, then we'll be on our way.'

Ford's body seemed to heave with relief at having saved the horses as Quint pulled tight on the rope around the cowboy's ankles.

'What's that?' said Seth, spying the edge of a white card protruding from the chest pocket of Ford's shirt. He poked at it with Henry's Colt. 'What have you got in there?' he asked. He pushed his free hand deep into the pocket then pulled out a neatly folded package wrapped in paper.

Quint pulled the rope tight around Ford's chest as Seth holstered the handgun and began to unwrap the paper. It was all the money that Ford owned in this world, neatly folded and bound by the list of provisions he had purchased in Sedalia. When Seth saw the money he let out a whistle. 'We've hit the jackpot with this one.'

65

'Let me see.' Quint's eyes opened wide.

'Better than that other one; he had next to nothing. Has this one got any more?' Quint was now pulling at the other shirt pocket, bunching in up above the bands of rope.

'There ain't no more,' said Ford.

Seth slid the neatly folded bills into his own jacket pocket, opened the list, examined it for a moment or two, then let it drop to the ground. He then turned over the last remaining item, the card. 'What's this?' He said as he gazed upon the postcard.

'It's Madam Marie Rosine,' said Ford.

'And who's she when she's at home?' asked Quint looking over Seth's shoulder.

'She is an opera singer. An angel.'

Quint grabbed the postcard from Seth's dirty fingers. 'An angel, eh?' He examined it closely, leering at the image. 'Well let's see if she can fly.' He turned the card lengthways in his dirty fingers and ripped it in two, slowly, then four, just as slowly, then eight before he threw the pieces high into the air. Ford looked up and watched as a light wind caught each ripped portion to spin and flutter them across the desolate prairie, to fall at last upon the dirt.

'Why did you do that?' asked Ford. 'It was just a photograph, of no importance to you.'

Seth leant in close to Ford, who felt the sour breath upon his face. 'Because we can, see, and nobody is going to stop us. Not you, not nobody. That's why.'

Ford looked down at Henry's handgun, the grip protruding from holster with the letters H.O. for Henry Owens. 'The man you took that from, is he dead?'

Seth pulled the Colt from the holster. 'Nice, isn't it.'

Ford asked again. 'Is he dead?'

'Not yet,' said Seth still looking at the gun in his hand. 'But I don't know about tomorrow.'

'Where is he?'

'A day from here but he's not going anywhere and nor are

you.' Seth laughed and did a little jig in front of Ford as Quint pulled hard on the rope around his boots to check that the knots were tight.

As the sound of the clanking tin pans slowly faded, along with the sight of the wagon and his two horses now tied to the rear, Ford's free hand was frantically pulling at the tight, hard knots, while his thoughts filled with frustration and anger. He was annoyed at himself for being jumped, for being robbed, again, and especially for the destruction of his beloved postcard of Madam Marie Rosine. But he also thought about Henry. What had happened to him? Was he still alive? And why was he just one day behind him? Was he trying to catch up and if so why?

It took just over an hour before Ford's numb fingers felt the hard rope ease just enough for him to push the the tip of his little finger into the small opening.

'Come on Ollie,' he called out to the silence. 'You got to do this or you are going to die out here like a dog.' He pulled at the rope, straining muscle, bone and sinew as he let out a howl. A small loop opened a little further, so he let out another howl, long, like a coyote, as he pulled at the rope, now widening it just enough to push his thumb through the small gap. 'Yeowl, yeeowl, yeeeowl,' he called. He twisted and writhed on the ground, kicking at the dirt and howling like a wild dog until, just after sunset and near exhausted, he finally felt the end of the rope pull free by just an inch. But here was a sign that gave him the hope and confidence that he could get free.

18

PEBBLES

It was pitch dark when Ford slowly stood, then stumbled, fell, stood up again and kicked off the loose rope from around his boots, and cursed. His fingers were blistered and numb from the constant pulling on the stiff twine, and his limbs were sore from where they had strained against the tight bindings. He ran his tongue across dry lips, swallowed and cursed again.

He searched around for any items that the muleskinners might have left. But he found nothing of use, just some small cleaning cloths and a small brass bottle of oil for his now stolen weapons, along with a piece of pumpkin and the ripped tatters of his beloved postcard. He looked everywhere for his hat, at one stage getting down on all fours to look low across the ground in the hope of seeing its dark shape against the night sky. But it couldn't be found and he knew it was time to go.

Ford figured that he was fifty miles from Red River, a two-day easy ride, but on foot how long would it take? He guessed that he might be able to walk at two and half maybe three miles an hour, about the same speed as the muleskinner's wagon. He even thought that he might be able to catch up to them, if they stopped and rested the mules, but then what? He had no weapon.

Ford cussed aloud. Got to get to Red River, he told himself. Once there he could explain to the authorities what had happened. But how long would that take? If he walked hard, non-stop, no rest, he could be there . . . when? He quickly calculated in his head – within twenty-four hours. 'I can do that,' he said as if having a conversation with himself, just as the light from the moon pierced through the clouds to reflect upon the barren ground. Ford turned to take one last look for his hat and saw the marks of the wagon tracks, now clearly visible, their parallel lines stretching away to the south and easy to follow. Ford turned slowly on the spot, searching for his hat as his eyes caught sight of the tracks to the north, to where Henry had been bushwhacked.

'One day away,' he mumbled. 'They said one day.' Ford looked north, thinking. One day of travel, during daylight, what would that be, twenty, twenty-five miles? How long on foot, ten to twelve hours? But what then? If he did find Henry they would be seventy to seventy-five miles from Red River. Ford turned and looked south, then north, then back down south again.

Henry will be fine, he told himself and stepped off to the south, striding out in long deliberate steps, counting, while a small worm in his ear repeated, Henry will be fine, Henry will be fine. But before he got to one hundred steps, he stopped. 'Damn,' he said, then turned and faced north. Will Henry be fine? He knew how lucky he had been to get out of his binds. Had one hand not been left free for him to sign the papers for the bogus sale of his horses he would have had no chance to pull on that first knot. He'd still be hogtied, rolling around on the ground and in trouble – deep trouble. 'Damned rattlesnakes and muleskinners,' he yelled at the top of his voice before he stepped off again, but this time he was heading north and once again he began to count.

Ford counted each time his left foot struck the ground and after 1,000 left footsteps, he picked up a small pebble and dropped it into his empty left pocket. That first little pebble represented approximately one mile in distance. It was a trick that Mr Dennison had shown all the cowhands at Waco. 'It's rough but good enough to measure any distance that you need to. Keep it up your sleeve,' he had said.

Ford reached down, without breaking stride, scooped up some more pebbles, dropping all but one into his right pocket. The one that he retained he rolled between his thumb and forefinger as he counted his steps, his boots crunching upon the hard, dry dirt. At the count of 1,000 he dropped it into his pocket to clink gently against the first pebble. He had now covered two miles.

The crumpled bandanna that was usually stuffed into his left pocket he now tied around his neck to mop the sweat that was starting to glisten upon his skin in the moonlight. And when he dropped the tenth pebble into his pocket he guessed it might be about midnight or maybe a little later, as the moon was now directly overhead. If this was correct he had now been walking for about four or five hours at two or maybe two and half miles an hour.

The parting cloud let the light of the near-full moon shine like a lantern, clearly showing the straight lines of the wagon tracks. 'If you can keep this up, Ollie,' he said out loud, 'you'll be close to Henry by first light.' But two hours later Ford knew he was slowing down. His right hip had started to ache and his feet were starting to feel as if they were on fire.

Another two hours on and he was now walking with a hand pressed to his hip, in the hope that it would ease the dull pain. A little later he took a rest, sitting upon the wagon track and pulling off his boots. As he rubbed his feet for relief and opened his toes to let the air circulate, he closed his eyes, just for an instant, to rest.

How long he had been asleep he didn't know, but the moon was now low and dawn was approaching. He could see the glow of dawn across the horizon and cursed as he looked up, his neck stiff from where his head had awkwardly hung while he slept. He had lost valuable time, time for cool walking.

The ground crunched under tired feet as he desperately tried to get back into a rhythm, transferring the pebbles back from his left pocket to his right. When the sun rose its heat was

70

instant upon his face and scalp, so he took the bandanna from around his neck, tied a knot in each corner and pulled it over his scalp. By mid morning ths sun's rays seemed to be burning a hole in the top of his head, especially when he placed his hand upon the surface of the red bandanna. So he took off his shirt to make a cloth cap, leaving the tail to hang back over his neck and on to his shoulders. Then he tugged at the sleeves of his woollen combinations, pulling them up each arm to expose the skin to the air as he continued the silent count to each step of his left foot upon the ground.

The next five miles were slower again and harder than before as Ford squinted into the heat haze, his mouth dry and water a constant thought. When he pulled the pebble that marked the twenty-fifth mile from his pocket he stopped. The muleskinners' tracks continued to stretch out before him into the shimmering heat, a desolate place with no sign of life. He turned the small pebble over in the clenched palm of his hand, then rubbed it between his thumb and finger while he looked at the northern horizon, which appeared to float in the heat and glare. He was now seventy-five miles from Red River, weary, without water and worried. Very worried.

19

ONE MORE MILE

'Henry where are you?' The words from Ford's cracked lips were barely audible. 'Come on, Henry give me some sort of sign, I'm almost spent.' But there was no answer to his plaintive call and the only movement to be seen was the constant shimmer of heat. Ford looked down at his dirty boots to rest his

71

eyes, then back up into the fierce hot landscape. 'One more mile, Henry, that's all I can give you, no more.' He stepped off, and as his left foot struck the ground he began a fresh count.

When he dropped the pebble into his pocket one mile later he stopped in a scuff of dust, exhausted, searching for sign, dead or alive. Some birds circled high directly in front of him, but they were beyond any distance he could bear to think of. He looked down at the wagon wheel tracks, then lifted his eyes again. 'Maybe,' he said in a whisper, 'I can give you one more mile but no more, after that I have to try and save myself.'

A half-mile on and the wagon tracks turned sharply to the right, then disappeared as they dropped down into a dry creek bed and over a flat rocky course. Close in towards the far bank, where the wheel ruts were at their deepest, the sun flashed from the ground to blind Ford. He turned his head from the glare before glancing back. It flashed again.

It was a small but long muddy puddle with patches of cream coloured scum upon the surface. Ford closed his eyes, frightened to open them, just in case it was a mirage. He edged forward, his foot slipping and twisting on the hot smooth surface of the rocks, before he squatted down next to the tiny pool and dipped his fingers into the water. It was hot but it was wet. He pulled the shirt from his head and then the bandanna from his neck. He dipped it into the pool and placed it in his mouth. It moisture was warm and he could feel the sand and grit on his tongue and teeth, but he sucked hard on the wet cotton, then dipped it back into the water and sucked again, dipping and sucking, dipping and sucking.

This wretched little sump, this squalid little drain, this dirty little water hole was a reservoir of life and Ford knew it. But he wondered whether it was just delaying the inevitable; by his calculation he was now twenty-six and half miles from where he had been bushwhacked and seventy-six and half miles from the Red River Station. If he walked at two and half miles an hour without a rest, it would take. . . ? His mind wasn't working. It would take. . . ? 'Come on, Ollie,' he called out. 'Think. It will take . . . thirty hours.' His head dropped. Could he possibly endure thirty more hours?

A heavy weight formed in the pit of his stomach. He knew he couldn't walk at two and half miles an hour for thirty hours. Even two miles an hour would be an effort, as he needed to rest for at least five to ten minutes after each hour. So in reality he was at least forty hours away from comfort, from safety, from survival. He dipped and sucked on the rag. Forty hours! He hung his head, pushed the rag into the muddy puddle and started to feel the overwhelming weight of defeat. Forty hours! He closed his eyes and felt the tears well. Forty hours!

The flap of wings pulled Ford back from his deep black thoughts, it was behind him, and when he turned he saw the small beady eye, then the grotesque red neck and large hooked beak of the vulture. It had landed on the edge of the dry river-bank and had come for water, but Ford thought it had come for him. He seized a rock to throw but it was too hot to hold and he lost his grip as he threw. The large bird turned its head as the stone skidded by but it didn't move.

'Get,' Ford called but it sounded more like a croak. 'Get,' he tried calling again. 'You're not getting me yet, buzzard.'

The bird stood still and watched, prepared to wait.

Ford waved his shirt in the air.

The bird looked mildly interested, then tilted its head as if amused at the proceedings.

'Not yet,' said Ford. 'And not before I finish having my ablutions.'

Ford pushed his shirt into the middle of the hole, which was surprisingly deep, coming halfway up his arm as the shirt disappeared. He pulled it out, twisted off the excess water back into the pool, held the shirt open as the slightest of breezes stirred the air to cool the moist fabric. He then laid it across his face and head with the tail falling on to the back of his neck.

The coolness upon his skin was a soothing joy. He lifted the shirt to the sky to let the air pass over the wet cloth again, then dropped it back over his head, while the buzzard watched, some fifteen paces away. Each time the bird came back into view as Ford lifted the shirt from his eyes and held it aloft, and it was then that he saw the thin piece of meat hanging from the beak. The bird had come to drink after a meal.

The realization was savage. Had this bird come from feasting on Henry's horses, or from feasting on Henry?

Ford stood, then lurched, his feet uneven on the rocks, to stumble towards the bank then up to the wheel ruts, to stand and look north. He glanced back over his shoulder at the bird, which now hopped two or three steps towards the water hole. He looked back along the wagon tracks. 'Come on, Ollie. For Henry, just one more mile.'

20

78 MILES

Ford rolled the little pebble in his fingers as he counted, his left foot scuffing the ground as it barely lifted above the baked dirt. His left boot had taken 947 shuffling steps, 948 pathetic little steps with a foot that felt like it was on fire, 949 steps that had each stabbed a pain up the length of his leg and into his hip, 950 left footsteps from the water hole. Fifty more and he would arrive at the end of his last mile. The one more mile that he had promised Henry. One mile on from the muddy puddle, twenty-seven and half miles on from where he had been robbed and left for dead and seventy seven and a half miles away from Red River Station.

The ground quietly crunched under Ford's boot as he came

to a halt. He released the pebble slowly to let it fall to the bottom of his pocket as he searched the horizon through tired, burning eyes. He slowly shook his head. He could see nothing, just a bare horizon, shimmering in the heat haze.

Ford looked down to the ground to rest his eyes. Just then he heard the swooshing sound of a bird's large wings as it passed to left, the shadow of the buzzard gliding over the ground, heading north, its silhouette precisely framed between the wheel tracks of the wagon. He watched, mesmerized by its shape, its ease of travel over the ground, effortless and elegant.

He lifted his eyes to sight the bird, its wings spread wide as it slowly descended, then dipped to one side to turn in a tight circle and finally land on what seemed to be a small, dark mound. Ford looked, straining to see, the shimmering heat of the late afternoon sun obscuring his view of the dirty brown landscape. Was it a rise? A rock? Was it?

'Horse.' The word came from dry cracked lips that hardly moved, a murmur to no one but himself. 'It's a horse.'

Ford stepped off, forcing himself forward, looking, searching with each step as his eyes fixed upon the dark object in the distance. Each step brought him closer to where the bird had landed, each step came a little more quickly, his eyes probing the heat haze, each step now shuffling to the hiss of his trousers as the fabric brushed between his legs. Then he saw it, the out-stretched leg pointing towards the low sun. A thin leg from the black, bloated body of a dead horse; it was now a gruesome perch on which sat the vulture as it watched Ford scurry forward, almost tripping over his feet.

Directly behind the first horse was the carcass of a second. Both were bloated black and lying in a small depression, the wagon wheel-marks passing close by and continuing north.

'Henry?' It was no more than a croak from his parched throat. 'Henry?' Ford turned, looking, searching for some sign of the marshal. To his left was a small, shallow, dry creek bed. He shuffled down the low bank and on to the soft sand to glance along the dry watercourse. He saw the heel of a boot close in to the bank. He went to run forward but the soft sand was heavy underfoot and he tripped and fell.

He looked up and saw legs tied and roped. 'Henry!' He crawled forward on all fours, his eyes now able to see more of the bound figure, the rope around the unmoving torso. 'Henry,' he yelled as he placed his hand upon the body and felt the cloth of the jacket warm from the sun. Ford crawled in closer to see the head pressed hard against the bank in the little shade that was cast.

Ford felt the air suck hot into his lungs as he grabbed at the body, his fingers trembling. Henry's face was pressed into the sand of the riverbed and it was difficult to turn him over, so he pushed his hand under the side of the face and gently pulled it around expecting the worse. Just as the mouth came clear of the sand, a small cough came from the lips.

'Henry,' called Ford.

A second cough. 'Ford?'

'Yes it's me. Ollie.'

'Ollie, how the hell,' the words were laboured, 'did you find me?'

Ford held Henry's face as he spoke, keeping the lips from the sand. 'One of the muleskinners had your handgun. I saw your initials on the handle, so I came looking for you.'

'You did that? You did that for me?' The words were slow and soft.

Ford nodded.

'Was it hard to find me?'

'Hell no,' said Ford sarcastically in an attempt to sound like Henry. 'Real easy.'

Henry coughed again. 'You want to untie me or are we going to stay like this?'

Ford pulled his hand away quickly and Henry's face fell back into the sand as Ford's fingers moved to the first bunch of knots and began to work frantically.

Henry lifted his head with difficulty to speak. 'They shot the horses.'

Ford kept pulling on the knots. 'I know.'

'When I find those rattlesnakes I'm going to kill them.'

'We got to get out of here first.'

Henry's right hand came free and he slowly flexed his fingers, the stump of his missing finger waving about. 'I could have got out if I had all my fingers. I was almost there.'

Ford kept pulling at the tight knots and hard rope around Henry's legs. 'Yeah, I noticed.'

Henry's left leg was now free and he drew it up towards his chest slowly as he tried to sit up.

'Here, let me help.' Ford eased Henry into the sitting position.

Henry straightened his leg. 'You are going to have to help me up on to your horse. I'm seized up here.'

'What horse?'

Henry looked at Ford with concern. 'They didn't shoot your horses too, did they?'

'Nope.'

'Thank God for that.'

'I gave them to them.'

'What?'

'Either that or they were going to kill 'em.'

'So you gave them away?'

'Yep.'

'So how did you get here?'

'I walked.'

'You walked? How far?'

'I reckon twenty-eight miles.'

'How do you figure that?'

'I measured it.'

'How?'

'Pebbles.' The rope was now coming free as Ford pulled it through the mass of knots and from around Henry's arms.

'Pebbles? So how far have we got to go?' asked Henry.

'To Red River? Seventy-eight miles, I guess.'

'Seventy-eight miles? You think we are going to walk seventy-eight miles back to Red River.'

Ford pulled the last of the rope free and threw it behind him. 'You got a better idea?'

'I was just asking you for help to get on a mount. I doubt if I could walk a mile at the moment.'

'Well, you have to walk a mile and half back to the water hole.'

'You found a water hole? Praise the Lord for that. What's it like.'

'It's an oasis Henry. The only thing it hasn't got is a palm tree.'

'Really?'

'No. It's a wheel rut, but it's a wheel rut with water in it. Now, try standing up.' Ford put his arm around Henry's back to help him to his feet. Henry stumbled. 'Come on, Henry, you got to get up.' Ford pulled and slowly Henry stood.

'Hat, I got to find my hat,' said Henry.

'I can't see it. They took mine and I think they took yours too.'

'I'm going to kill those snakes.'

'That's the spirit.' Ford kept his arm under Henry to keep him from falling over. 'Anyone who steals a man's hat deserves to die. Now try walking a little.'

Henry stumbled forward to the edge of the small sandy bank and looked across at the bloated carcasses of his two dead horses. 'Just help me up the bank, then I should be OK.' Ford eased his shoulder under Henry's arm to assist him up the bank. 'You reckon seventy-eight miles to Red River then?'

'That's what I figure.'

'And a mile and a half to water?'

Ford nodded.

'Then when's the next water after that?'

78

'Nothing between there and where I got bushwhacked.'

Henry caught his breath as he got to the top of the bank. 'And that's fifty mile from Red River?'

'The way I reckon it.'

'Then we better pray that we find water early on in that last fifty miles or we won't make it.'

'That's what I figure too but I try not to think about it.'

Henry gave a little nod then croaked through cracked lips. 'Yeah, I can see why.'

21

A STROLL IN HELL

The sun had set by the time the two pathetic figures arrived at the water hole.

'Where's the palm tree?' mumbled Henry as he continued to dip his bandanna into the muddy pool and suck hard on the dirty wet cloth.

'I lied,' said Ford.

'Did you lie about the distance too, or is Red River really just over the hill?'

Ford looked south over the flat landscape. 'No, it is close to eighty miles away.' He then added the word, 'unfortunately.'

'Let's not add one more inch than we have to. You said this water hole is seventy-six and a half miles from Red River, so that hill will be just over seventy-six miles away, not eighty.'

'Right,' said Ford as he took the brown soaked bandanna from his mouth.

Henry removed his jacket and pulled his shirt from his back. 'I'll show you a trick,' he said and submerged the shirt into the little stagnant pool, screwed it out squeezing the water back into the pond, shook it open in the air then dropped it over his face. 'Old Indian trick,' he said from under the wet fabric.

'I didn't know Indians wore shirts.'

Henry didn't respond to Ford's observation. 'Try it, it will revive you.'

'I did exactly that on my way to find you.'

'You learn it from an Indian?' asked Henry.

'No. I learnt it from my mother. She used to cool us kids down in the Texas heat with a wet cloth.'

Henry had tilted his head back and the wet shirt outlined the features of his face. 'Maybe she learnt it from the Indians.'

Ford smiled, just a little. 'Henry, what were you doing following me?'

Henry remained silent.

'I said—'

'I heard.'

'And?'

'I was worried about you. So I thought I should tag along and make sure you didn't get into any trouble.'

'I see,' said Ford.

Henry was nodding his head under his wet shirt as if to confirm the story to himself.

'Wasn't very successful though, was it,' observed Ford.

'Not all plans work out exactly,' said Henry.

'Could be worse,' said Ford.

'Really?' said Henry. 'How do you figure that?'

'We could be lost.'

'I've never been lost,' said Henry.

'Never?' asked Ford.

Henry lifted the shirt from his head, waved it in the air and dropped it back over his head. 'I may have been geographically embarrassed once or twice in difficult country but that would have been some years ago when I was as young as you are now.'

'Right,' said Ford. 'Geographically embarrassed a long time

80

ago.' He dipped his dirty red bandanna back into the pool. 'Well, this time we know where to go, so all we have to do is just get there but with no prospects of water once we leave here. So, do we stay here and drink this pond dry, first?'

Henry pulled the shirt from his head. 'If it was whiskey I'd say yes but this is far from whiskey.'

'Well, we should start as soon as the moon is up and we can see the tracks. And,' said Ford, 'once we start, I don't believe we should stop. We should just keep walking, no matter how tired we get. If we rest I think we will—' But he didn't finish.

'You reckon we are seventy-six and half miles from Red River Station?'

'That's what I calculate, from this water hole, by my count.'

'And how long do you think that will take?'

'If we can average between two, and two and half miles an hour, then around thirty-five, thirty-six hours.'

'And,' said Henry, 'twelve hours of that is going to be through the heat of the day?'

Ford nodded. 'The bit in the middle.'

Henry threw his wet shirt back over his face. 'That'll be the bit that's a stroll through hell.'

'Do you think we can make it, Henry?' Ford's voice was quiet and showed his concern.

'Hell no,' said Henry. 'But we can die trying.'

Once again Ford smiled, just a little, because it was good to be back in Henry's company.

The light was not as bright as it had been the previous night as wisps of cloud passed over the face of the moon. Ford walked along the left wheel track and Henry along the right, eyes down cast to check that they were on course for Red River.

The light got a little better as the moon rose higher, and when it was overhead, Ford calculated that they had covered close to fifteen miles.

'Be there in no time,' observed Henry in his drawl.

Ford repeated back, 'No time at all.' He was certainly feeling better, at least in his mind, than he had been the previous day. He put it down to the muddy water hole, the cool air and not being alone. The ache in his leg and hip seemed to be no more than a nuisance that could be forgotten, especially when he let his mind wander or when he silently took small pleasure in reflecting on the success of his endeavour to find Henry.

But their pace slowed as the night wore on, step by step along the wagon tracks, and it was well after sunrise when they arrived at the spot where Ford had been bushwhacked.

'I expected to be at least three to four miles further on by now,' said Ford.

'When I'm walking it always takes me a little while to get into my stride,' said Henry. 'I expect that I'll speed up near the end. A little like a racehorse.'

But Ford didn't smile at Henry's humour this time. His thoughts had shifted to the agony that lay ahead. He pulled off his shirt and wrapped it around his head. 'You might want to do the same and get rid of your jacket.'

'My coat?' said Henry. 'I've had this coat for years. It's a good coat. I bought it in Chicago.'

'Well, maybe it's time to get a new one, because it will be too hot to wear or carry.'

'We'll see,' said Henry.

By mid morning, Henry was still carrying his coat, looped over one arm, transferring it from time to time from the left to the right and back to the left arm again. An hour later he said to Ford. 'I think you're right, maybe it is time for a new jacket.' He opened the coat up, removed his badge and put it in his trouser pocket. Then he lifted from the inside pocket a small sheaf of papers tied by a thin dark-blue ribbon, before dropping his jacket to the ground.

'I'd throw those away as well,' said Ford glancing at the papers in Henry's hand.

'Can't do that. These are legal documents. They give me the

authority to go after the preacher and his two idiot sons.'

'I can't see that being of much importance at the moment.'

'Importance? These papers got you off the hook in Sedalia. If it wasn't for these,' Henry shook the sheaf at Ford, 'You'd be sitting in a cell right now for wilful murder and contemplating the end of your young life.'

'Can't you get new ones when we get to Red River?'

'Would take months. Warrants for the apprehension of a man, dead or alive, take time,' said Henry as he stuffed the bundle inside his sweat-stained vest.

For the next five miles the ground became very soft and sandy under foot, which slowed them considerably. So by the time the sun was directly overhead and another pebble fell from Ford's fingers to the bottom of his pocket, it marked just the thirty-sixth mile since they had left the water hole. 'Got just over forty to go,' he said. 'But we aren't yet halfway there, we should be at least half way by now.'

Henry's voice was faint and he didn't turn his head as he spoke. 'We'll get there when we get there.'

But the air was now oven-hot from the sun that beat down upon the two shuffling figures with their shirts tied around their heads, to provide some modicum of protection.

The continual steps, the constant plodding, the counting each time the left foot struck the ground, the moving of pebbles from one pocket to the other, and the endless gaze upon the wagon tracks was constantly accompanied by a terrible thirst. Their minds might have wandered and drifted to other thoughts in a feeble attempt to find a better place but the attempt never, for an instant, dislodged the craving for sweet, cool, clear water.

Ford would close his eyes and drift for a glorious second or two, his mind remembering the rivers and streams he had played in as a youth, before snapping awake as his feet stumbled. When he opened his eyes it felt as if they had been filled with fine-grained sand, and when he blinked it was with irritating discomfort. It was all he could do to keep his hands from rubbing deep into the sockets in an attempt to gain a little relief. But it was his head that hurt the worse. The light, dozy feeling that had been with him for the last two days had now been replaced by a throbbing ache at the base of the neck.

The only consolation seemed to be that the ground was now becoming firmer underfoot, baked hard by the sun. However, by mid afternoon they had covered just five more miles and still had thirty-five to go.

'You see behind us?' mumbled Henry.

'What?' Ford had trouble comprehending.

Henry twisted his shirt-covered head slightly to the rear. Ford glanced back to see a thin dark line of cloud.

'That's rain,' said Henry.

'Where's it heading?' said Ford in a whisper.

'You want to know where it is heading?'

Ford nodded.

'I have no idea and I'm not going to think.'

But thinking was what they did – deep, dark thoughts of despair that begged the body to surrender and give up. Even when the sun finally set, it brought no sense of relief. By now they had descended into a trance.

Ford swallowed hard, his mouth dry. 'Thirty miles to go.'

Henry slowly pulled his shirt from is head. 'I've got to rest, just for a little.'

Ford looked at Henry and was shocked at what he saw. The marshal's bearded face, covered in dust that seemed to glow from the last light of the sun, was lined and drawn. But it was his eyes. They seemed to have retracted into his skull to become small and dark, giving him the look of a defeated man.

'We can't, Henry. If we stop we will never get started again. Our bodies will seize up. If we stop we die.'

Henry was silent as they trudged on for a quarter of a mile, then he spoke. 'Maybe it's best you go ahead and save yourself.'

'No,' said Ford, surprised at the power of his voice. 'No Henry. We have less than thirty miles to go.'

'I'm spent,' said Henry.

Ford shuffled in close to the marshal and put his shoulder under Henry's arm to support him.

Henry tried to push him away. 'You can't carry me for thirty miles. You go on.'

'No, Henry. We can do this. We are close.'

'But not close enough,' mumbled Henry.

'Yes we are. We are almost there.'

'You know, Ollie, I've never been a quitter but this is too much for me. I haven't got thirty miles in me.'

'But we've done the hard part,' argued Ford. 'It's getting dark. Come on, Henry, give me one more mile, just one more mile.'

22

THE ANGELS SING

It was now pitch black with the moon low in the sky and obscured by heavy cloud.

'We're travelling blind, Ollie. We are going to lose the wagon tracks.' Henry's voice was no more than a whisper.

Ford was defiant. 'If we stop we die.'

Henry's voice was laboured. 'If we lose the tracks we die.'

'If we lose the tracks we can still head south to the Red River, then go west to the station. There's water in the river; we'll be OK.'

Henry turned his head so that it was close to Ford's ear. 'But do you know which way is south when you can't see your hand in front of your face?'

They trudged on in the dark, then Ford stopped abruptly. 'We'll rest but as soon as we get some light from the moon and can see the tracks we must push on.'

Henry didn't answer; he just let out a grunting sound as Ford eased him down until he seemed to collapse into the ground.

'That was three and half miles. We're only twenty-six and half miles from the station. Just fourteen hours away.'

Henry rolled back to lie upon the ground, the air from his lungs exhaling to sound like a sigh of relief. 'We're not four-teen hours away from the station. Not with you dragging me along like you've been doing. The last mile was slow, very slow, I counted.'

'We'll be faster after we rest,' said Ford. 'You'll be able to walk OK.'

'Ollie, I've had it. I'm spent. I just want to lie here and die in peace.'

'We can't do that.'

Henry's breathing was shallow. 'You can't but I can.' He spoke slowly. 'You press ahead as soon as you can see those tracks and leave me be.'

'I won't do that,' said Ford. 'We've come this far. We're almost there.'

'Twenty-six and half miles is not almost there. It's a day's ride for a man and a horse, with water. Two men on foot with no water . . .' Henry paused to get his breath. 'It's impossible for me but maybe not for you. But if you try dragging me along, then you'll die too.'

Ford was shaking his head with frustration. 'I'm not going on my own. We either go together or we stay here.'

'To stay here is to die.'

'Well, so be it,' said Ford.

Henry was silent for a long time. Then he propped himself up slowly on his right elbow. 'Isn't that what you said before you shot Zachary Hayes? So be it.'

Ford looked towards his feet and could just make out the shape of his boot in the dark. 'Yeah, something like that.'

'Where did you learn that? "So be it". I like that. Was it from your schooling?'

'My mother use to say it.'

Henry repeated the words slowly. 'So be it.' Then he said. 'You ever been scared, Ollie?'

'Sure.' Ford's voice was soft.

'When?'

'Roping cattle for Mr Dennison.'

'Scared how?'

'Scared I'd let him down and make a fool of myself. Mr Dennison took me on when there were far better men than me around.'

'No, I mean really scared. Scared for your life? Like when you shot Hayes. When you went searching for me.'

'Yeah, sort of.'

'Has it ever stopped you from doing what you needed to do?'

Ford thought for a moment or two. 'No, I don't believe it has.'

'I guessed as much.'

Henry eased himself down to lie on his back once again. 'When a man still does what needs to be done, when he is scared to his back teeth; then he is no coward.' Henry rested his arm across his eyes but kept talking, slowly and softly. 'When you came back for me, you knew it could lead to this but you came back anyway.'

Ford didn't say a word.

'I would have liked to meet this Mr Dennison; he must be a good judge of horseflesh because there are no men better than you. And believe me I know. I may have seen a lot of the riff-raff in this world but I've also met some good men, especially during the war, and you measure up to the best of them.'

Ford remained silent.

'But now you've got to save yourself. My time has passed and I thank you for coming after me. It gave me the chance to get to know you a little better.'

Ford sat hunched and quiet in the dark of the cool air as it shifted on the breeze from his face to his back, becoming stronger and humming through the small dried tuffs of needle grass around him. He closed his eyes and the feeling was wonderful, like drawing up a down blanket on a cold night in the knowledge that a comfortable sleep lay ahead.

A flash of brilliant light bought him to his senses and he wondered if it was a dream. It happened again and he saw Henry, just for an instant, lying on his back, both arms now drawn up and folded across his face as if to shield his eyes. Then a crack of thunder split the air like the crack of a whip, to be followed by a second high-pitched crack as the wind began to howl. More lightning flashed to light up the barren wasteland like day, to be quickly followed with blasts of sound, close and threatening.

Ford stood up slowly to look for the wagon tracks as the sky lit up with another flash of lightning. He thought he could make them out, over to the left, but wasn't sure. They had wandered away from their lifeline and he began to feel panic. Lightning flashed again with the sound of the thunder now almost at one with the spectacle, as Ford continued to search for the tracks. Then from behind him came a roar that engulfed and confused his senses. He turned as the sky flashed bright blue and that was when Ford saw it: rain. Streaks of vertical silver-grey rain, a wall of falling water riding on the tail of a strong wind that now raced towards him.

The first drop struck his right cheek with a sting, to splash water into his eyes. The second and third fell on his head, hard, big, round, full drops of thunderstorm rain. The roar was now getting louder as it marched towards him with speed – wild and fierce and he could smell it, fresh, clean and sweet. He closed his eyes, tilted his head back and opened his mouth as the torrent swept over him.

The rain was so heavy that his mouth filled in seconds. He swallowed, each mouthful cool and satisfying. Am I dreaming? he thought as he cupped his hands under his chin to collect more water and drink. 'Henry,' he called. 'Henry.'

Ford crouched down next to Henry and lifted his head and shoulders up. Henry leant back on his elbows. 'Open your mouth, Henry,' yelled Ford as he cupped his hand under Henry's chin to funnel the cascading rain across Henry's lips. 'Can you hear it, Henry? It sounds like a marching army.'

Henry nodded. 'It sounds like,' he said between mouthfuls of water, 'angels singing.'

23

DROWNED RATS

The downpour continued, constant and heavy during the night, as the lightning show travelled south to entertain with its display of fireworks. The falling rain quenched their desperate thirst and refreshed and cleaned their stained clothing from the white salt sweat marks upon their backs. It also washed away the dust and dirt that had covered every part of their bodies from collar to cuff; and the acid urine smell and stains where Henry's had relieved himself when hogtied, and the blood-stains low on the seat of Ford's striped pants. All had now been laundered by nature as the two men sat, contented as children in a splashing puddle that collected to swirl around them as if they were upon a seashore on a holiday. The water also seemed to clean away the despair that had been heavy upon their minds, as the cool sweet smell of the rain chased away the whiff of death that had been present just hours before.

As first light appeared over to their left with its grey streaks under heavy, low cloud, Ford eased himself up, first on to his hands, then to his feet. The rain was lifting from a steady drizzle to a light mist that made the air moist to breathe. When he looked south he could see the wagon tracks glistening in the early light as two long thin streams leading to Red River Station like a silver trail to salvation.

'We can go now, Henry,' he said with his eyes fixed on their destination.

Henry pulled himself upright with a grunt and Ford knelt to put his shoulder under his arm.

'No,' said Henry. 'I'll do this myself, at least for the next twenty-six and half miles; after that I may need a hand.'

Ford smiled but said nothing to Henry as the two shuffled forward across to the wagon tracks to begin their plod, splashing through the water in silence.

The now wet and soggy landscape no longer seemed hostile. It had turned into a very different place from the one they had been shuffling through the day before. The colour of the sky was dim, replacing the bright, burning sunlight, and the oven-hot air was now a gentle, cool breeze that blew over the sheets of water lying in patches upon the once-hard dry ground. This place had been transformed from a hell into a scene of heavenly neutrality.

Ford's feet no longer burned but squelched, his shirt was no longer hot and sticky but wet, cool and heavy on the shoulders. His body still ached, especially his hip, and his legs felt as heavy as lead, but his mind was light and he felt his back straighten as the moist air lifted his chest with each breath. He cast a glance towards Henry, who also stood straighter as he ran a hand over his hair, pushing it back from his forehead to flatten it over his neck to the collar.

'How do you feel, Henry?' asked Ford.

Henry kept looking straight ahead, his face grim with determination. 'I feel great; can't you see that?'

'Of course I can, Henry.' The reply was spoken with conviction and agreement. 'Of course I can.'

By midday they had sludged through nine miles of waterlogged landscape. By mid afternoon they had covered another four saturated miles, and by nightfall another three and half, leaving them just ten miles from safety.

As they trudged on into the dark they lost sight of the track but kept walking in silence, in the hope that they were still heading south. But with each step Ford became a little more concerned. They were so close but now they were travelling blind for the first time on this perilous journey. So it was with enormous relief that he heard the sound of rushing water straight ahead, just before they abruptly arrived at the eroded banks of the Red River in full flood.

'Red River,' said Henry. 'It's the Red River.'

Ford looked down from the sandy edge of the bank at the dark menacing flow. 'If we had fallen in we would have drowned.'

'Is that such a bad way to die?' said Henry.

'For me it is,' said Ford as he watched the mass of heaving water. 'So all we need to do is follow the bank up to the crossing.' Ford's voice showed renewed enthusiasm.

Henry gave a grunt, then stretched out a hand and placed it upon Ford's shoulder. He gave two pats and mumbled something, but Ford couldn't hear what was said as the sound of the river drowned out his words. He thought he said 'thank you', but he wasn't sure and he didn't like to ask. So, he just turned and started to walk beside Henry towards the crossing. Two men, who had cheated death by determination and good fortune; two men walking side by side, their shoulders almost touching.

*

It was just after midnight when they caught sight of the oil lamp through the branches of the river trees. It seemed to drift like a low star in the night, never getting closer until at last they were upon it. It was a miserable little light, hanging on a narrow porch, dim with just the moths orbiting around the dirty glass chimney for company.

The two men stepped up on to the creaking planks and stood before the door.

'After you,' said Henry.

Ford knocked on the old rough door, then stood back to wait. He was ready to knock again when the door slowly scraped open to reveal an old man dressed in a nightshirt and with concern on his face.

'Excuse me, sir,' said Ford. 'Is this Red River Crossing?'

'Two mile down.' The old man showed that he was reluctant to come out.

'And Red River Station?'

'Two mile across the river, in Texas. But you can't cross tonight, not after the rain we've had. Come out of nowhere it did,' he said.

'And us,' said Henry, to announce their arrival in his commanding voice that Ford hadn't heard since they were both back in Sedalia. 'But we have travelled far and hard, and need to rest. As law-abiding men may we lean on your good nature.'

The old man seemed to respond, as if he was now in the company of an important person. 'Sure,' he said. 'You boys hungry? I'll open my store. I got some chilli I can warm and I can make coffee.' Then he added. 'But you'll have to pay.'

'Sir,' said Henry. 'I am a US marshal and this is my deputy. We were bushwhacked by rattlesnakes, but through the grace of God we have managed to survive. Your comfort is gratefully received and will be paid for as soon as we find the thieving dogs who waylaid us.'

The old man now turned to look at Ford with a little confusion on his face. Ford extended his hand. 'Hi, I'm Ollie, pleased to meet you. We'll get you the money but we will have to owe first.'

The old man nodded with reluctance, then pulled hard on the door. It scraped upon the floor as it opened a little further. 'So you boys can pay, then?'

'Not now but we will pay,' Ford reaffirmed.

'You look like two half-drowned rats.'

'We feel like it, too,' said Ford. 'But we're not complaining. We kinda like the rain.'

The door jerked open a little more. 'Bring in the lamp so I can light up inside.'

Ford put his hand up to the old bent wire handle but it was hot, so he pulled the cuff of his shirt down over his fingers and lifted the little light down from its nail hook.

'You have a sheriff here?' asked Henry as they entered, to find that they were in a small settlement store but one where most of the shelves were bare.

'Sheriff Boyd Munroe from the station is here. He's staying down at the crossing. Got caught this side by the flood. No one can get across at the moment. Even the ferry.'

'So he's a Texan?' said Henry. 'But what about a sheriff for this side of the river?'

'Not one this far south, not since the tornado wiped out most of the settlement. The closest law is at Chickasha and he is busy looking after the Indians, so we don't see him much. If we need the law we talk to Sheriff Munroe.'

'Is he a good man?' asked Henry.

'He's fair and straight, I guess. Likes being in charge and he knows the law. He was practising to be a lawyer before he became sheriff.'

'Really,' said Henry, pulling a face that showed disapproval. 'A lawman that was once a lawyer, now that sounds precarious.'

24

THAT'S THE LAW

'I can take you in to the settlement to see Sheriff Munroe but it will cost you.' The old storekeeper was reheating the last of the beans for breakfast. 'Or you can walk, it's only two miles.'

Ford and Henry each stole a glance at the other, walking another two miles hurt just thinking about it. While Ford's sleep upon a horse blanket on the floor of the hut had been sound, he had woken weary and with aches in every bone of his body.

'That will be fine,' said Henry with his air of command. 'Just add it to our bill.'

The three rode up front on the hard bench seat, side by side, with Ford in the middle as the old wagon jarred and creaked along the riverbank at a walking pace towards the crossing. The clouds had lifted but they were still dark and threatening as the cool air upon Ford's face helped to remove the fuzziness he felt in his head. He tried to remember the country from when he had crossed with his team on the journey north to Sedalia, but that now seemed an age ago and back then the river had been low and the sky a clear blue. Another reason why it looked different was also upon Ford's mind, as he knew he was seeing things differently now, as if for the first time. He certainly felt older and a little wiser to the ways of the world, and in some respects a little less fearful – but not of all things.

When he had crossed the river on his trip north it had been with a strong degree of trepidation that had only evaporated when he arrived safely on the other side, for he had a dread of river water. In fact, he hadn't slept a wink the night before that crossing with the cattle, preferring to remain on watch in the hope that he could keep his mind away from what lay ahead.

As a boy of seven he had come close to drowning when he had foolishly investigated the trunk of a tree that had fallen into the river. One foot had slipped off the trunk while his other had got caught in the branches, holding that leg high out of the water but his head below the surface. It had happened in an instant, taking him by fright and giving him no time to cry out.

Had it not been for his sister's presence and quick response he would have drowned. She had come to the rescue and hauled him out by his hair. Then she had scolded him with a fierce tongue. That lasting impression of being trapped and fighting for air between mouthfuls of water remained a recurring nightmare to this very day and one that could wake him in a sweat.

When he had crossed the river on the journey north, he had done so with these still vivid memories, and white knuckles that gripped at the horn of the saddle so that he would not become separated from his horse.

The main crossing point, the one used to get the herds across the Red River, was on a sharp bend where the watercourse turned north before meandering on east. Further back upstream from that point was a small settlement of timber and tarpaper buildings used by those who worked the old cable ferry. This was known as the crossing and was used as the everyday method of crossing the river with dry feet. It had once been a busy and industrious place but the demise of the Red River Station had taken its toll. The ferry, like the buildings at the crossing, had seen better days but it was still serviceable and large enough to take a wagon with its team and some additional horses and passengers besides. The little supporting shantytown also provided rough overnight accommodation for those who were caught on the wrong side of the bank when the river flooded and needed to wait until a crossing could be made.

On the other side of the river lay Red River Station, some two miles south on a tributary called Salt Creek. It was surrounded by good cattle country but its reason for existence had little to do with grazing and everything to do with the crossing. It marked that point where the cattle trail left Texas territory then split to go due north to Kansas or north-east across to Missouri.

As the wagon pulled in next to the first shanty the old man pointed to three men grouped together and talking with their heads down, studying what seemed to be a chart. 'That's Sheriff Munroe in the middle,' said their host.

Henry squinted in an effort to recognize the fellow-lawman who was tall, clean-shaven and neat. Henry's study included a long look at his polished boots, which were shiny against the mud upon the ground. Henry let out an 'oomph' sound that Ford interpreted as disapproval.

The sheriff glanced up at the wagon, made note of what he saw, then returned his eyes to the map.

Henry and Ford dismounted and stood, waiting for an opportune time to introduce themselves, but it didn't seem to come in a hurry, until the sheriff eventually turned and said, 'Can I help you boys?'

Henry was ready. He held his badge up in his hand to display the star with its silver crescent. 'I'm US Marshal Henry Owens and this is my deputy, Ford Tate. We are on federal business, chasing down the murderers of a federal judge, but in doing so we fell foul of two bushwhacking muleskinners. We seek your assistance.'

The sheriff stepped forward. 'Only too happy to help a federal officer but legally there is little I can do while on this side of the river. This is Indian territory; my patch starts across the river in Texas.' He looked Ford up and down as he spoke, then cast his gaze back on to Henry. 'What sort of help are you after, exactly?'

'Have you seen any muleskinners in a wagon of late? We have followed their tracks south to the river.'

'One is called Quint,' added Ford. 'They have two horses with them, hitched to the back of their wagon.'

'I've seen them,' said the sheriff. 'Spoke with them the day before yesterday. The ferry took their wagon across the river and as far as I know they are down at the station. They were fixing provisions before heading south to Fort Worth. They were trying to sell the two horses.'

'Well then,' said Henry, 'if you can loan us some weapons and assist us to the station, we'll go and retrieve our belongings.'

'And how do you propose to do that?' The sheriff's tone and stance, with his foot forward and thumbs in his vest pockets, made him look more like a lawyer or alderman than a lawman.

Henry glanced away, a little confused with the question, then answered. 'By killing the rattlesnakes, of course.'

'I can't let you do that. Not unless you've got papers.'

'I do have papers,' said Henry, 'but for a different matter. I have the papers for the apprehension of one Jacob Hayes, who calls himself The Preacher, one Joshua Hayes and his brother, one Jonah Hayes.'

'I know them too. Came through three days ago, heading south. You better let me see those papers.'

Ford looked at Henry with surprise on hearing the news that the Hayes had passed through the crossing just three days ago.

Henry didn't respond to Ford's look as he pulled the wad of papers from inside his shirt. He then slowly untied the ribbon and tried to peel back the first sheet of paper. It started to separate in his hand. It was sodden with water.

'I need to be careful,' said Henry.

'I can see that,' said the sheriff as he leant in close to look.

Henry gently lifted back the page to show a mass of smudged blue ink stains upon the saturated document.

'I don't think anyone can make head nor tail of that now,' said the sheriff. 'You can try to dry it out but I think it is well and truly ruined. You may have to send for new papers.'

'That will take too long,' said Henry. 'If they are just three days ahead we should make haste.'

'It doesn't matter how much haste you make. Without the papers you can't force an apprehension. If you end up in a shoot-out you could find yourself on the wrong side of the law.'

'I am the law,' said Henry. 'I'm a federal marshal and I have been sent to apprehend these men. Each of them has a bounty on his head, and I mean to get—' He stopped abruptly, then corrected himself. 'I mean to enforce the law.'

'But you can't do that without the papers,' said Sheriff Munroe. 'Not here, not in Texas, not anywhere. That's the law.'

Henry looked around as he stuffed the wet papers back into his shirt. 'So what help can we get from you, Sheriff?'

'Well, you can let me do my job. Later today these two gentlemen,' the sheriff glanced over his shoulder at the two men behind him who had been listening into the conversation with interest, 'hope to make a crossing with the ferry and I plan to be on it. I will then speak to the two old fellas at the station who, you say, took your possessions, but I will need detailed statements from you both as to exactly what happened. And in regard to The Preacher and his boys, well, I'll send a telegraph to Austin advising of the situation.'

'We'll come with you,' said Henry, more than a little agitated. 'Then I can deal with those bushwhacking rattlesnakes.'

'No,' said the sheriff. 'Best you stay here. If there has been a transgression of the law they will be held and I will call for you.'

'Transgression of the law!' said Henry, now clearly annoyed. 'Those thievin' vipers hogtied us and left us to die a merciless death.'

'Well that's yet to be proven one way or the other but at the moment all I see before me is two lawmen who are alive, if maybe a little wet and worse for wear.' The two men behind the sheriff gave a gentle laugh. 'All I ask is for a little patience and tolerance, while I look into this matter,' concluded the sheriff.

Ford could clearly see that Henry was now angry.

'Well, patience and tolerance were never my best virtues,' said Henry.

'What are, then?' asked the sheriff.

'Shooting straight and retribution. Those rattlesnakes may not have killed us but that was only by the grace of God and a thunderstorm. I don't know how many other bodies those two have hogtied and left out on the prairie to die of thirst, but as sure as hell I'm going to make sure they don't leave any more.'

'I think you might be getting het up,' said the sheriff.

'Het up? Damn right I'm het up. I was expecting to kill two vipers, not sit around discussing the finer points of Texas law.'

Ford remained silent, watching, his eyes glancing back and forth as each spoke, while wondering: is this how lawmen conduct their business with each other?

25

DEPUTY TATE

Ford was reluctant to bring up the subject, especially now that Henry was clearly in a bad mood. But as the two men sat under a mesquite watching the red muddy swirls of the river dip and heave with the heavy flow, there wasn't much else to talk about.

'Henry, why did you tell the sheriff I was your deputy? You said the same to the storekeeper.'

Henry had pulled some bark from the old tree and was examining it closely as he mumbled something, but Ford couldn't understand what he was saying over the sound of the river.

'I'm sorry, Henry, I didn't hear what you said.'

Henry turned the bark over in his hand and mumbled again.

'I'm sorry?' repeated Ford.

Henry looked up. 'Damn it Ford, I've got a lot on my mind.'

Ford wouldn't let this one lie. 'I'm sure you have, but if you want me to be your deputy then you need to explain how this works.'

Henry's shoulders relaxed and he casually threw the bark away. 'I think you and me make a good team.'

Ford nodded. 'I do too, Henry.'

'After all, we have been through a lot together of late.'

Ford nodded again.

'And I may need a hand or two to finish this job off, especially if Texas is full of lawyers turned lawmen. It could be more than handy to have a good man by my side.' Henry leant forward and picked up a thin stick. 'Truth is,' his voice now had a serious tenor, 'I'm not getting any younger and while experience may make for a full hand most of the time, luck still plays its odd card. This will probably be my last job and the trick is, to get out of this business before your luck runs out.'

Ford chose not to ponder on this declaration by Henry about his age, past good fortune and future chances. 'Can you make me your deputy?'

Henry was flicking the end of the stick against the ground but on Ford's precise question as to the mechanics of making him a deputy, he threw it away to end his brief spell of introspection. 'Well, by the law you need to be sworn in by a judge. But there is a provision, when in the field, whereby goods can be commandeered for use in the course of the administration of the law.' Henry's pronunciation was now clear, no mumbling; he was quoting the law by rote in a tone of authority that was the mark of US Marshal Henry Owens. He picked up a second stick, shorter but thicker and held it upright in his fist like a sceptre, as if to mark his authority. 'And I believe this rider could be extended to people.' Then he added. 'Of sorts,' and lowered the stick.

Ford wasn't sure what Henry was saying other than, yes, in a legal sense it could be done, but in the process he would also be classified as goods, which seemed OK, he guessed. 'I'd like that, Henry,' he said. 'I'd like that very much.'

Henry looked up with surprise, threw the stick away, and extended his hand for Ford to shake. 'Well, Deputy Tate, let me welcome you to the US Marshal Service.'

Silence once again fell upon the pair as Henry looked around for another stick before eventually settling on a piece of rough bark from the old mesquite tree.

'Henry?'

Henry didn't answer as he leant forward, picking up the bark and bringing it to his nose to smell.

'Henry, were you surprised that the Hayes had crossed through here just three days ago?'

Henry began to examine the bark closely, rolling it over in his hand as he mumbled something, but again Ford couldn't understand what he was saying over the sound of the river.

'Henry?'

Henry remained silent for a little, then he shrugged and said, 'I guess.' But he didn't look Ford in the eye when he spoke.

26

THE LAW AND JUSTICE

The sheriff returned the following day and Henry was anxious to see him, standing close to the riverbank, below the cable that tethered and guided the old ferry to the shore. The sheriff stood next to his horse and waved from the timber decking of the ferry, but only Ford waved back.

As he soon as he stepped off the ferry the sheriff began to talk. 'I took the liberty of sending a telegraph to Austin to seek information on Preacher Hayes and his two sons but I am yet to receive a reply.' He was now close to Henry. 'I'm sure Austin will seek advice from Washington and respond within the week.'

'Within a week!' mumbled Henry. 'They could be in Mexico within a week.'

The sheriff seemed to take no notice of Henry's remark. 'As for the other matter,' he said. 'I have spoken to both Seth and Quint and they showed me a bill of sale for the horses. All looks above board.'

Ford stepped past Henry towards the sheriff. 'I only gave them a bill of sale to stop them from shooting the horses. They shot Henry's.'

'Well, that's not what they are saying and they have the papers to prove it.'

Henry had his hands on his hips and was shaking his head. 'Those papers were signed under duress, in order to save two fine horses. You let me talk to them and I'll get you the truth.'

'Well, I can't do that now.' The sheriff looked a little coy. 'They decided to leave last night.'

'What?' said Henry in a bellow that surprised both Sheriff Munroe and Ford. 'They did *what*?'

'Well, I had no reason to hold them. They were going to stay, then after I spoke to them they decided it was time to leave.'

'I bet they did,' said Henry. 'They'll be heading down the Chisholm to get away like it was a Roman chariot race track. As soon as they knew we had survived and were at the river they would have cacked themselves knowing we were after their hides.'

Ford now put his hands on his hips in frustration. 'They have our guns, provisions and my two horses. So what do we do now?'

Henry looked around before he spat towards the river. 'Don't know, but we can't stay here.' Henry looked directly at the sheriff. 'I'm going into Red River Station and I guess I'm going have to walk. But once I'm there I want a little assistance from you.'

'Sure,' said the sheriff, now somewhat chastened from Henry's outburst. 'Only too happy to help.' Then he added: 'Where I can, but we must let the law take its natural course. It is not just man's will but the will of the good Lord.'

Henry's face seemed to set hard, except for his eyes that narrowed with disagreement. 'Are you a church man?' he asked.

'Yes I am,' said the sheriff with pride.

'Well, let one old lawman give another lawman a little advice. Don't let your Christian goodwill get in the way of justice.'

The sheriff had an earnest look on his face. 'But the law of the land and the law of God are at one.'

Henry's face twisted as he moved his mouth about before he replied, showing that he didn't like being interrupted. 'I'm not talking about the law, I'm talking about justice, and the law and justice are not always at one with the other.' The sheriff went to speak but Henry would have none of it. 'I will need money to send a telegraph direct to Washington explaining the situation. My deputy and I will need a place to sleep and we have no money for meals. I want to run up an account with you until such time as you can be reimbursed by the Department of Justice.'

Henry would have kept on talking, but the sheriff interrupted. 'The Department of Justice? Don't you mean the US Marshal's Office.'

'No,' said Henry. 'I have been see-conded,' he drew the word out in his Southern drawl, 'from the US Marshal's Office to the Department of Justice. This is a federal matter as it involves the killing of a federal judge.'

The sheriff rubbed his chin in thought and it seemed that

those four words, The Department of Justice, were a key to unlock the sheriff's previous reluctance to help. 'I see,' he said as he continued to rub his chin. 'And who would that judge be?'

'Judge Harris of Ashville, North Carolina. Shot six times and left to die in front of his grandson who was in his pyjama suit.'

The sheriff let out a long low whistle. 'In his pyjama suit, eh?'

'That's right,' said Henry. 'That is the sort of rattlesnakes we are dealing with here. Vipers portraying themselves to be men of God when they are in fact Satan's servants.'

The religious aspect of Henry's sermon seemed to reinforce for the sheriff the urgency of the situation, as he responded by saying. 'I'll walk back to the station with you.'

'So you will help?' said Henry.

The sheriff nodded. 'Of course, the Department of Justice can depend on me.'

'Good,' said Henry with authority. 'You can start with payment of the storekeeper who fed and brought us into the settlement.'

27

THREE TELEGRAPHS

The cable ferry was a rickety affair that had long seen better days. Its planks had split and lifted from years of sun and rain, and the low railings on each side had been tied and retied with rusting fencing wire in a vain attempt to offer some protective barrier. However, merely to touch the dilapidated banister would seem enough to send this arrangement of sticks collapsing into the torrents of the Red River.

The ferryman pushed hard on the pole to start the journey and ease the flatbed out into the river from the embankment. The boards under the passengers' feet moved and creaked as the strong flow took hold of the brittle vessel trying to push it sideways downstream. The ferryman withdrew the long shaft from the muddy bottom; cast it on to the weathered deck with a rattle and ran to the ropes that tethered the vessel to the overhead cable. The heavy sisal lines now pulled and strained, calling a start to their voyage as the heavy block and tackle flicked in the air, to dance below the overhead cable. With a wave of his hat the ferryman signalled to the far bank and a team of oxen began to pull. Slowly, very slowly, the old flatbed barge began to inch its way across the swollen river.

The strong current lurched the ferry to the creak of shifting timber, which caused the sheriff's horse to flash white eyes and lift its head in fear.

'Steady,' said the sheriff. 'Gets a little nervous when we use the ferry and the river is in flood.'

'Me too,' said Ford quietly as he positioned himself in the centre of the deck and next to the horse. If this bunch of sticks and aging driftwood goes down, he thought, I'm hanging on to the horse.

As Ford pressed himself close to the belly of the mount, his hand on the stirrup, Henry and the sheriff seemed oblivious to Ford's concerns, standing side by side as they spoke. When the ferry nudged at last against the far bank, the cowboy felt a great sense of relief. He was the first to put his feet back on to dry land.

The walk from the ferry to the station was just on two miles, southwards along the bank of Salt Creek, which was flowing strongly into the river. The track was serviceable but muddy, exposing some large rocks where the water had washed down the wheel ruts. Each muddy puddle looked friendly to Ford's eye while the sheriff did his best to make careful steps around them to keep his boots clean and dry.

Red River Station, like the ferry and the settlement, had also seen better days and was showing its age. Some of the buildings were deserted and had been boarded up giving an impression of bleak weariness. Ford had not bothered to go into the station on the journey north; he had had no need and the herd had been marshalled close to the river for the crossing, a mile and half away. Mr Dennison and cookie had gone in to replenish the supplies, and when Ford had asked cookie what it was like, the old man had just shrugged. Ford now knew why.

When they arrived at the sheriff's office and the sheriff took his horse to the stalls at the rear, Henry grabbed Ford's arm.

'He won't budge,' he said softly as if passing a secret. 'I hounded him to give us guns, ammunition and horses so that we can chase down those two muleskinners but he'll have none of it. Says if we kill 'em he will be an accessory by supplying the means to commit an offence. What offence shooting two hogtying rattlesnake muleskinners would be, is beyond me.' said Henry shaking his head. 'Seems they have some strange laws in Texas.'

'So what do we do now?' asked Ford.

'I'm going to send off three telegraphs. The first to Washington to advise that I have crossed into Texas and intend to travel south towards Austin in pursuit of Hayes and his boys. The second, to ask for the State Department to advise the State Office of the sheriff in Austin that I am heading their way with orders to apprehend Hayes and his boys for the wilful killing of a federal judge. That should overcome the difficulty of the spoilt papers.'

Ford waited for Henry to continue but he seemed to fall into a trance, deep in thought and staring at some distant unseen point.

'And the third?' asked Ford.

'Humph?' came the sound from Henry as he came back to life.

'The third telegraph? What is the third one you are going to send?'

106

'Oh,' said Henry. 'That I have deputized Olford Tate, a citizen of Texas, for the purposes of assisting me with the apprehension of Hayes and his boys, dead or alive.'

The meaning of the words and tone in which Henry said them, using his authoritative voice, came on to Ford with a weight that now seemed to rest on his shoulders like a heavy hand.

'I won't have a badge to give you but that's no matter. It is the permission that counts; you understand, don't you?' said Henry.

Ford no longer felt the years that separated them in age or the experience that Henry had over him. He felt like an equal partner in a grand enterprise. 'Yes,' he said, 'I understand.' But it came from his lips as if someone else was speaking the words, someone who knew what lay ahead. But that was something Ford had no knowledge of whatsoever.

28

BROKEN AXLE, BROKEN LUCK

When Henry returned from the telegraph office he set about searching the station for horses, guns, ammunition and supplies but all turned up short.

The only horses good enough for a long ride south belonged to the sheriff. An inspection of the stables showed it to be near empty, as his two deputies had taken six horses to patrol downriver and would be gone for the next three weeks. The situation with firearms and ammunition was even worse. The keeper of the general store said that he used to stock both until the tornado had hit the town some four years before. Now there was no need for such items. 'I am,' so he said with the resignation of a defeated man, 'running down my stock until I have nothing left worth selling. Then I'll leave.'

The fierce storm some years before had been a windy death knell for the station. Nearly half the folk who had called Red River their home had used its passing to decide that it was now time to go South. The reason wasn't solely the damage from the big blow. A rumour that the Missouri-Kansas-Texas Railroad was not going to run their new track through Red River Station but further south left many of the business owners in a quandry.

'When that happens it will be over for this town,' said the shopkeeper.

To Ford it looked like it was over already.

'I can sell you boys some of the essentials though. I've got flour, a little sugar, coffee and salted beef but the only weapons I have for sale are two derringers and some hunting knives.'

'What are you doing with derringers out here?' asked Henry, his tone showing that he felt it was a foolish notion to stock such a puny weapon for those who rode the range.

'Bought them in for Roaring Nettie and her girls at the Crimson Curtain. They liked to be armed but concealed. When the Crimson Curtain closed, they left and, well, nobody else had a need for them. Pity, beautifully made. I can let you have them cheap.'

Ford examined the two little handguns. The embossing on their silver frames was indeed finely crafted. As he held one of the pistols in his hand he was surprised by its weight and balance.

'Now,' said Henry in his voice of authority as he took the gun from Ford's hand. 'They can be lethal but you have to know how to use them.' He pulled the squat double barrel up on its hinge and looked into the small chambers, then clicked it back on the frame before he held the muzzle close to Ford's head, near the temple. 'The range is short so you need to get as close as you can. Aim where it will produce a fatal wound, so the head should be the prime target. Preferably the side or back.' He moved the muzzle around to the back of Ford's head. 'I saw a man shot in the stomach with one of these.' Henry now tossed the small gun up and down in the palm of his hand. 'It was in the hallway of a boarding house in Conway, Arkansas. He was a big man, filled the hall from side to side with his girth.'

'What did it do to him?' asked Ford.

'Made him as angry as hell.' Henry laughed and so did Ford and the shopkeeper, but Henry continued to laugh long after they had finished, enjoying his humour with a deep belly-laugh as water filled his eyes.

At least, thought Ford as he waited for the laughter to finish, Henry is well and truly back in the land of the living.

Late in the afternoon a small herd of cattle, less than 200 head, grouped tight and on their way north to Abilene, arrived and parked themselves at Salt Creek in preparation for the crossing of Red River. It was the lead group of a larger mob that had separated and pushed two days ahead of the main herd, which had got caught on the wrong side of a swollen creek down near Bowie.

Ford saw the two young cowboys with the older man, who, he guessed, was the team boss, standing by the counter in the general store selecting provisions from a small list. The cowboys were in training and under the guidance of the older man, and for a moment envy crossed Ford's mind as he stood and looked at the three deep in conversation. When the older man looked up at Ford, he gave a smile along with 'howdy' and Ford felt obliged to converse, but before he could speak the team boss asked whether he was heading north or south.

'South,' said Ford, who then asked, 'Is the going good?'

'It'll be fine in a day or two. Dries out quick. Just need to scout around the puddles but watch out for those puddles.' He gave a Texas smile and the two cowboys grinned. 'We came across two old muleskinners who got caught in one and did in an axle.'

Ford felt the breath suck back into his lungs and he stopped short from letting his eyes widen with surprise. 'Are they OK?' he asked, slowly.

'Sure, they are fine. We offered them a ride back into the station but they were keen to keep on their way.'

'So, they have moved on?'

'Not when we left. The whole rear axle has split lengthwise so the wheels have tilted in and are scraping up against the sides of the wagon. I can't see them going anywhere soon.'

'So when did you see them?' Ford tried to keep his voice casual.

The team boss turned to the two cowboys. 'What time was that? Close to midday. Maybe a little before.'

The cowboys looked up and nodded in agreement, then went back to looking at the list that lay on the counter.

'So,' said Ford. 'That would be about . . . how far back?'

'Oh, five or six miles. No more.'

Ford held on to his breath and did his best to look casual. 'Well, I do hope they are able to fix their wagon.'

'Me too,' said the team boss. 'You know what they say. A broken axle – broken luck.'

Ford wanted to say something smart but nothing came to mind, only that he needed to see Henry quick. Real quick.

29

GET OUR HATS BACK

Henry paced up and down on the narrow porch of the sheriff's office. 'Five or six miles they said?'

'Yes, that's what they said.' Ford sat on a small bench, leaning forward, legs apart, elbows on his knees and his hands gently clenched just below his chin.

'Saw them today?'

'Close to midday.'

'Broken axle?'

'Broken axle,' repeated Ford.

Henry turned and paced back. Ford watched.

'Do we tell the sheriff?'

Henry stopped abruptly. 'Nope,' he said, loud. Then he started pacing again. 'He's gone back across the river and is of no help on this matter.' He looked towards the river, then mumbled, 'Or any other matter.'

'So what do we do?'

Henry stopped his pacing and ran his hand over his head, pushing down the hair and leaving his hand on the back of his neck. 'Damn. Those snakes are just down the road apiece but they may as well be in Jericho.'

'Why?' asked Ford.

'Why?' said Henry, drawing the word out long. 'Because we don't have any horses or any guns to kill those rattlesnakes, that's why, Ford.' It was said with condescension.

'So we walk. We could be there in two to three hours. If we hurried along, even less.'

Ford's solution seemed to take Henry by surprise and he stopped pacing. He then took two steps and stopped again. 'We've got no guns.'

'We could take the derringers, be nice and easy to carry.'

'Derringers!' Henry was dismissive. 'Then what?'

'Well,' Ford was thinking as he shuffled his feet. 'It will be in the dark, so we could creep up on them, slowly, get in close.'

'And do what?'

Now Ford was starting to get a little annoyed with Henry. 'We could get my horses back. Get my money back, and our guns, and our bedding, our provisions, or at least what's left of them.'

111

Then Ford said. 'Get our hats back too.'

Henry lowered his hand from the back of his neck. 'You know, it's just silly enough to work.'

'Well, if it doesn't then it doesn't,' said Ford. 'But at least we will have tried, instead of just sitting around here waiting for a telegraph.'

Henry thought for a moment or two. 'OK,' he said in a voice of authority. 'Let's get this stunt under way.'

Henry tried to act nonchalant as he leaned against the shopkeeper's counter. 'Those derringers,' Henry waved a hand towards where they lay on the shelf. 'You know, if the price was right, we might take them off your hands. Could be a handy gift to give out this coming festive season. A little trinket for a lady friend or two.' He waved his hand again, then added. 'For the right price of course.'

The shopkeeper could smell a sale. 'I could do the two for forty-five dollars.'

Henry put on a pained expression, as if he had bad indigestion. 'These are small guns and that's a big price.'

'Nettie and her girls were paying that each and I can't go any lower.'

The pained expression on Henry's face was now showing severe heartburn. 'I don't know.'

'I'll throw in two boxes of ammunition, one for each gun.' The storekeeper leant down under the counter, then came up with two small boxes of .44 cartridges.

'You're a persuasive man,' said Henry. 'Put it on the sheriff's account; we are his guests while on official business for the Department of Justice.' Henry showed his US marshal's badge.

'Well, I don't know.' The storekeeper was hesitant.

'I will sign any appropriate bill of sale,' said Henry.

The words seemed to have the desired effect and the storekeeper slid his hand along the counter to grasp the invoice book as he pulled the pencil from behind his ear.

Henry looked up at the wall behind the counter, which was

cluttered with an array of goods. 'And you better give us two canteens, with shoulder straps.'

The storekeeper turned, stepped up a small ladder and pulled down two water canteens. As he did so, the empty space on the peg revealed a large knife in a tan leather sheath.

'And that,' said Henry. 'You better give us one of those as well. It could come in handy.

'It's a good big knife,' said the shopkeeper as he pulled it from the hook on the wall.

'I know,' said Henry as he looked down at the little guns. 'May need it if we've only got these peashooters to depend on.'

'What was that?' said the storekeeper as he stepped down off the ladder.

'I said, a good knife is a handy thing to have.'

'Well, this is a good knife and the last one like this that I have in stock.' The storekeeper pulled it from the leather sheath to expose the large silver swordlike blades. 'Sixteen inches of fine Pennsylvania steel and as sharp as a razor.'

Henry looked closely at the knife, which reflected his unshaved face in the wide blade, and smiled. 'Yes sir, now that is a knife to be proud of.'

30

FIND A ROPE

They had been walking for just over an hour when Ford dropped another pebble into his pocket. 'That's three miles.' He could feel the ache in his hip slowly returning and he gave it a rub with the palm of his hand.

Henry was silent except for the gurgling sound that came

from his lips against the spout of the round water canteen as he drank.

It was now dark, with no moonlight to assist them, but the track was clearly marked and the land gentle, consisting of small rolling hills. Water still lay in the gullies but the ground was mostly firm under the foot. The only difficulty was sighting the odd rock that protruded from the wheel ruts. On more than one occasion the toe of a boot would catch and send the careless traveller forward in small scrambling steps, to save himself from falling flat on his face. When it happened to Henry it seemed to fire him up with great irritation towards the muleskinners, as if they had personally placed the rock to trip him up. 'I'll kill 'em. By God I'll kill 'em.'

This led Ford to question Henry on exactly what they were going to do once they caught up with the muleskinners.

'What do you mean, what are we going to do?' asked Henry in a hushed tone as they trudged in the dark. 'We are going to get back what belongs to us and wreak our vengeance.'

'How?' asked Ford.

'With surprise.'

But Ford had misgivings in regard to this enterprise. Although the two muleskinners had bushwhacked him, shot Henry's horses, and left them both for dead; he couldn't help but feel uneasy about the notion of killing them, especially in cold blood. The image of Zachary Hayes's face had been visiting him in his dreams again, uninvited; he now wanted to raise his concerns with Henry but couldn't quite figure how.

When the pebble that marked the sixth mile dropped into Ford's pocket they had been walking for well over two hours non stop. At the top of a small rise they searched hard for any sign of the wagon but found none.

'One more mile,' said Ford, so they walked on in silence.

At the end of that mile, Ford repeated his mantra of one more mile. But when that passed in silence and they stood upon another small rise, it seemed that their search for the bushwhacking muleskinners had been in vain.

'That's eight miles. Maybe they have managed to fix the axle.'

'Maybe,' said Henry, 'and maybe not. But they're not here, are they?'

'No,' conceded Ford. 'We could do one more mile.'

'No,' said Henry. 'My feet are starting to burn again and it's bringing back some unpleasant memories. We now have eight miles to cover back to the station and nothing to show for our endeavours.'

Ford took a swig from his canteen as they turned around and started back in silence, except for the tramp of their feet upon the track. It was almost exactly halfway between the sixth and fifth mile from the station, in a shallow depression where the warm air from that day had collected and pooled, that both Ford and Henry heard the sound. It came from the right side of the track, a metallic sound.

'Did you hear that?' said Henry.

'I did,' said Ford, looking into the dark. 'How far do you think?'

'Close. No more than one or two hundred yards.'

'Is it them?' Ford asked.

Henry pulled the small pistol from his shirt pocket, then the large knife from its sheath. 'If it is, they're dead.' He then seemed to weigh each weapon in his hands before shifting the pistol to his left hand and holding the knife in his right.

Ford watched for a moment, then drew his derringer from his pocket.

'Let's go,' said Henry. 'Time to skin us some muleskinners. Follow me.' Henry stepped off and Ford followed close behind as they started towards where they had heard the sound.

The ground dipped slightly, rose, then fell away again, while its covering was a patchwork of brush as tall as a man, providing cover from view for anyone who stood on the track. About a hundred yards in and some thirty off to the left was the unmistakable shape of a wagon.

Henry stopped and Ford drew up to his side to hear what he had to say. 'Stay in close to me,' Henry said in a whisper. 'We'll sneak in real quiet and take a look. If they see us, act quick and close fast and attack. If they start shooting we'll be in trouble as we are outgunned and a knife is no good unless you are close enough to stab or slash. So we need to be game.' Henry paused, then asked, 'You happy with that?'

It was then that Ford realized he'd just been given the plan of attack, but he wasn't sure what to say, so he just said, 'I guess so.'

About twenty yards out Ford could see the dim light of a turned-down oil lamp inside the wagon, which seemed odd as he expected the muleskinners to be sleeping outside, either close to or even under the wagon but not inside. He stopped Henry with a click of his tongue, then whispered in his ear. 'I thought only women slept in a wagon at night?'

'What?' came the low grunt from Henry.

'See the lamp inside the wagon?'

'I see,' whispered Henry, 'but it don't mean a thing.'

'We need to make sure, that's all. That we have the right wagon.' Ford's voice reflected his concern.

'Well, we can only do that if we go look and see.'

'Should we check under the wagon first?'

Henry was getting annoyed. 'Of course we should go and look under the wagon first. It's what I'm trying to do, so can we get on with it?'

They crept on, Ford still not sure that this was the muleskinners' wagon until he saw the outline of his two horses tethered to right. He clicked his tongue and pointed towards the horses. 'Mine,' he whispered.

'Right,' came the deep tone from Henry as he waved his knife in answer.

They were now close to the rear left wheel of the wagon and both stopped to listen, straining their eyes in the dark as they searched for the shapes of the sleeping men.

Henry took a step forward. Ford followed by taking one step. Henry took another step. Ford followed by taking another step. They were now alongside the wagon, between the front and rear wheels: two men, each with a tiny pistol in hand and one also carrying an oversized knife in the other. Two men who had cheated death and were now ready to take back what had been taken from them by two robbing muleskinners. Ford tightened his grip on the small pistol grip as he bent down to look under the wagon. As he did he heard the heavy snoring of two men from inside the dray.

As he stood to convey this news to Henry his shoulder caught on the side of a hanging pot, flicking it up in the air. It swung back on its hook like a pendulum to clang against a saucepan next to it. The metallic clatter broke the silence of the night.

Ford and Henry immediately lifted their tiny weapons, extending their arms towards the covered side of the wagon with its dim light, ready to fire at any target that now presented itself. But as the last pot came swinging to a rest, all remained still inside the wagon except for the heavy snoring that had alerted Ford to the occupants inside.

Henry glanced at Ford in disbelief, then slowly crabbed his way with small sidesteps to the front wheel. He slipped the knife into its sheath and climbed up on to the seat. Ford followed and was just putting his knee on to the seat when Henry announced, 'The jig is up and retribution is upon you, prepare to die.'

But the words were lost in the stillness of the night to be replaced by the continuing heavy snoring of those inside.

Ford pushed up next to Henry, then leant into the gloom of the wagon to see. He immediately coughed as a strong foul smell filled his nostrils. 'Jees,' he said. Then he held his breath.

'They're drunk,' said Henry.

Ford looked at the two bodies of the muleskinners sprawled

amongst a sea of trash and empty whiskey bottles.

'Drunk as skunks,' said Henry.

'What now?' asked Ford.

'Find a rope,' said Henry.

31

A POUND OF FLESH

The two muleskinners sat hogtied and fastened to the side wagon wheels, one to each wheel, their legs stretched out upon the ground, their hands tied behind their backs and their heads bare. Surprise at their captivity only came with their waking an hour before dawn from their deep drunken sleep. This had infuriated Henry, who had tried on several occasions to get them to a conscious state with a series of kicks and cusses. Ford thought that maybe they were hoaxing in a hope that they would be left alone without having to answer for their foul deeds, but that was never going to happen. Henry not only wanted to claim back what belonged to him but he also wanted his 'pound of flesh', as he told Ford.

While still dark, Ford and Henry began the search for their possessions under the dull light of the old oil lamp, but the mess within the confined space of the wagon had them tripping over each other, so Henry demanded that they throw every item from the wagon. Everything now lay upon the ground in a large heap. But apart from finding their saddles and guns, and attending to the horses, they could do little to recover the money and smaller items until the first light of day.

Henry also found an unopened bottle of Early Times Kentucky whiskey, which he began to drink. Ford abstained and

118

recommended that Henry do the same, but his protestation only met with a loud burp. With bottle in hand Henry kicked at the pile of junk from the wagon, while Ford picked up individual items for closer examination between the tips of two fingers as if they might be contaminated by a rare disease. 'I found my hat,' he told Henry, 'but I'm not too sure if I should put it on or not.'

'Something has died under this mound,' announced Henry as he took a mouth full of whiskey. 'I can smell it.'

Ford also found his jacket but it seemed to have something growing from a stain on the sleeve, which could have been rotten food, but precisely what type of food he wasn't sure. With the first streaks of early light they searched but found no sign of their money. Ford thought that maybe they might have a cash tin or some other such way of securing notes and coins, but no such container could be found. As Henry was taking another swig, Ford noticed the large number of empty whiskey bottles that now caught the glint of first light and it dawned on him where the money had gone.

'I'll have a small drink now,' he said to Henry.

'What made you change your mind?'

Ford put the bottle to his lips, took one mouthful, then handed it back.

'Is that it?' asked Henry.

Ford nodded. 'That's all I want, just one mouthful.'

'Why only one?'

'I just wanted to taste where all my money went.'

'What?' Henry looked baffled.

'Have you seen how many empty bottles there are?' said Ford, casting his eye over the pile of clutter at the back of the wagon. 'Because that's where our money has gone.'

Henry went to put the bottle to his lips but stopped and started to count the empties. The realization hit home. 'I'll kill 'em,' he bellowed and strode to the side of the wagon, drawing his reclaimed Colt with the initials H.O. as he went. 'Wake up,

119

you snakes, and prepare to meet your maker.'

Both the muleskinners remained still but Ford was sure each had dropped his chins upon his chest as Henry approached waving his handgun in the air.

'Rattlesnakes and muleskinners. I hate rattlesnakes and muleskinners and with these two we have both. So now is the time to rid the world of such vermin.' Henry stepped forward, pushed the barrel of his pistol against the top of Quint's head and took a swig from the bottle.

Quint screwed up his eyes, then called out, 'Don't shoot.'

'Oh,' announced Henry. 'The snake awakes.'

'I only did what Seth told me to do. Honest.' Quint pleaded with his eyes still squeezed tightly shut.

'Honest?' repeated Henry, pondering on the word. 'So then I should save you but shoot your partner?'

Quint said nothing.

'I can do that,' said Henry who strode across to the other tied figure and pushed the muzzle of his .45 against the top of Seth's head. 'Prepare to die, snake,' he proclaimed before putting the bottle to his lips again and draining it of its contents. He then threw the empty bottle to the ground, its glass clinking against the small stones as it rolled to a halt. Henry then wiped his left hand on his shirt and bought it to the grip of the Colt, so that he now steadied the pistol with two hands as he pulled the hammer back with his right thumb. The sound of the hammer clicked loud in the still morning air.

Seth's body started to quiver then his shoulders started to shake before he let out a whimper and wet himself. The smell of the urine puddle was pungent.

'Don't shoot him,' said Ford.

Henry turned his head to look at Ford who was brushing his hat with hand.

'Why not?'

'It would be wrong.'

'Wrong? Wrong?' Henry was bellowing again. 'What could

120

possibly be wrong with dispatching the likes of these two? Have you forgotten what they did? They stole our property, tied us up like hogs and left us to die a lonely and miserable death on the prairie.'

'But we didn't, did we? We are here and we have found most of what they took, except for the money.'

Henry looked confused. 'I know that, Ford,' he said, drawing out Ford's name as he tended to do when being contradicted. 'But that doesn't change anything; they still stole from us. Anyway, you shot Zachary Hayes for stealing from you, remember? I saw it. You shot him dead just like I'm going to do with these two snakes.'

'I didn't shoot Zac for stealing from me. I shot him for not giving my money back. Had he given back my money, then he wouldn't be dead.'

'Well I don't see these two varmints giving us back our money. So—'

'You didn't have no money anyway,' said Seth, who had decided it was time to join in on the conversation. 'The young one had all the money. You were bust.'

'I had some,' said Henry in defence.

'All you had was nickels and dimes.'

Henry became annoyed. 'Who asked you anyway?'

'I'm saddling up, Henry. We got most of what we came for. I'm leaving for Round Rock.'

'I still say we should shoot 'em dead.'

'And I don't.' Ford's tone was now one of authority.

'So how do I get my pound of flesh?'

Ford turned away and started walking towards the horses on the far side of the wagon.

'Don't go, mister,' pleaded Quint.

Ford stopped but only long enough to pick up his saddle and hold it across his chest before he continued down the small incline towards his two horses.

It was as he was lifting the saddle on to his horse's back that he heard the yell. It was a piercing sound of pain and anguish. He quickly pulled up and buckled the cinch strap, then turned and made his way back towards the wagon. He was almost there when he heard a second yell of pain. As he came around the end of the wagon he saw Henry with his large knife in his hand. The silver blade was red with blood.

'Shit, Henry what have you done?'

Henry was swaying a little. 'I got my pound of flesh.'

Ford looked down upon the two muleskinners; their faces were pale and contorted, their eyes wide and the sides of their heads pouring blood where Henry had severed an ear from each of the men.

'No more, Henry. No more. That's enough. We are not barbarians.'

Henry shrugged and slowly put the knife back into its sheath with his right hand. In his left he held the two ears.

Ford turned back to where he had recovered his possessions from the pile of debris at the back of the wagon and opened the blue covered package. He withdrew two menstrual pads, then returned to the muleskinners, placing a pad on each wound.

Henry watched in silence as Ford bound the improvised dressings to their heads.

'Saddle up the other horse, Henry, we're done here,' said Ford without looking up.

Henry gave a grunt, then sauntered away towards the horses. As he passed behind the wagon he threw the two ears on to the pile of trash and burped.

32

FOR YOUR SERVICES

The ride south was done mostly in silence. Ford didn't much feel like speaking and Henry didn't much feel like answering. At Fort Worth the sheriff told them that he had seen a preacher and his two boys; he couldn't recall exactly when, but he knew they were travelling under the name of Murphy, not Hayes. He also couldn't say where they were going in particular, other than south. Henry sent a telegraph to Washington, advising that he was heading south to Waco and would require money when he got there.

When Ford and Henry got to Hillsboro, they learnt that Preacher Murphy had actually hired a tent and had sermonized to a congregation on the Sunday. 'A true man of the Lord,' had said the post office clerk, as Henry handed across his telegraph to update Washington on his journey south. Henry responded with muttered disagreement under his whiskey breath, and a not so quiet profanity as he left.

At Waco Henry picked up the money order from the post office, which authorized him to draw one hundred dollars from the First National for expenses payable by the Department of Justice. He gave Ford thirty dollars at the bank counter before they walked over to the sheriff's office, only to find that the lawman had left for Austin City on government business, so they spoke to the on-duty deputy. He didn't know about any preacher, but yes, he had seen a man and his two sons travelling south.

'But you don't know where south?' asked Henry.

'Nope,' said the deputy, 'but I guess it could be Austin. If he is a preacher then there are a lot of church people who live in Austin. So, I'd say that, maybe, he's heading to Austin.'

Henry said nothing. But why should he? He knew where the preacher and his sons were heading, and it wasn't Austin.

While Ford was of half a mind to stay in Waco to try and find Mr Dennison, a voice inside told him to leave it and head for Round Rock. Besides, what was he going to say? And if Mr Dennison offered him his old job back he would have to refuse, and he didn't wish to show any disrespect by doing that.

Three days later at Georgetown, the sheriff there referred back through the daily reports to read out loud that Preacher Murphy and his sons had taken up a collection for the orphaned children of San Antonio from the people of Georgetown, while attending their end-of-summer picnic day.

'So,' said the sheriff. 'He must be heading south to San Antonio.'

'Now we know where they are going,' said Ford.

Henry held his tongue until he was out through the sheriff's door. 'They're not going to San Antonio and no orphan children are going to see a penny from that collection. They're heading to Round Rock.'

Surprise showed on Ford's face as he turned to Henry and asked, 'How do you know they are heading to Round Rock and not San Antonio?'

Henry became evasive but Ford persisted. 'Henry, how do you know that they are heading to Round Rock?'

Henry answered with a question. 'Well where do you think they are going?'

Ford thought for a little. 'Well, I had guessed maybe Mexico. To escape from the law.'

'They have no intention of crossing into Mexico. The pickings are too rich this side of the border.'

'Well then, why Round Rock or Austin or even San Antonio?'

Henry pulled his hat from his head and took in a full breath that swelled his chest. 'Because' – he glanced around before he looked back at Ford – 'because they are after you.'

'Me? They don't know me.'

Henry kept glancing around before fixing his gaze on Ford. 'Of course they know you. They know your name, they know your face, they know you killed Zachary Hayes and they know you are from Round Rock.'

'How do they know all that?'

'Because it's been in the papers and magazines. The illustrated ones too.'

'Yes but that was in Sedalia. They haven't been to Sedalia.'

Henry lifted his eyes skywards. 'The magazines go all over the place. The killing of Zachary Hayes was news, not just in Sedalia but also in Atlanta, Chicago and in Kansas City. I made sure it was news. I made sure they got to know that you shot Zac and that you were going home to Round Rock.' Henry put his hat back on his head. 'Damn it Ford, that's why I was following after you. As sort of . . .' Henry glanced around again 'protection.'

'I see,' said Ford.

'Damn it, Ollie, I had no other way of finding them. It was too good a chance to miss, you can see that, can't you?' Henry was now pleading.

Ford cast his gaze down the street, not wanting to look at Henry. 'Yeah, I can see.'

'But anyway, this was as far as I was going to let this stunt go.' Henry's tone changed to the voice he used when he took charge. 'I want you to wait here in Georgetown while I ride into Round Rock to get the preacher and those two idiot sons of his. And that is best done by me and me alone.'

'How do you figure to do that?' asked Ford. 'There are three of them and one of you. I thought I was your deputy.'

Henry nodded his head. 'That's true, but I don't plan to arrest them. Warrants have been issued on the heads of all three, dead or alive and I'm not going to take them alive, there's no need, and it's safer that way. When I find them, I will shoot them, dead, and I can best do that on my own. That way it will be over and done with. Be better for all.'

'Who's all?' asked Ford.

'The Department of Justice, the US Marshal's Office, every federal judge, the State of Texas, you' – Henry looked at Ford then slowly continued – 'me. All of us.'

'Well, I'm still going to Round Rock. It's where I come from.' It was said with defiance.

'I know that,' said Henry, as he put a hand on Ford's shoulder. 'But give me a twenty-four-hour start, that's all I need. You don't want to get involved in this, you're no killer.' Henry dropped his head just a little, the brim of his hat hiding his eyes, before he lifted it slowly to look at Ford. 'You're a cattleman. Give me twenty-four hours, then you come on in, after it is done and dusted, then I'll have some money for you.' Henry took in a breath. 'Money for your services to the office of the US Marshal, so that you may buy your mother a proper memorial stone.'

33

ROUND ROCK

By the time Henry was ready to leave for Round Rock, Ford had mulled long enough on Henry's plan that had seen him used as bait. Ford also had time to wonder: had he not come across the muleskinners and had they robbed and hogtied only Henry, then he would have continued on to Round Rock to ride unwittingly into an ambush. This brooding caused him to question the good judgement of Henry's plan and indeed the overall wisdom of all of his judgements.

As he lay on the cot of the Georgetown cell at the back of the sheriff's office, which had been provided for them as temporary quarters, his mind ran over exactly what might have happened. As he didn't even know what any of the Hayes looked like, he guessed that any one of them, or all three, could have walked up to him in the main street of Round Rock, surprised him and shot him dead before he even knew he was in danger.

That night he dreamt of being confronted and accused of killing Zachary Hayes by the preacher and his sons. In his dreams the preacher was a big powerful man dressed in black robes who spoke to a watching crowd, saying, 'What a fine, upstanding young man my Zachary was.' The crowd seemed to agree and one of them produced a rope from nowhere that looped effortlessly over his head, to be pulled tight around his neck. Fortunately, in this very same dream Henry arrived in the nick of time with not just one but two guns blazing, and yelling, 'Rattlesnakes and varmints. I hate rattlesnakes and varmints.' When Ford woke with a start it was not with relief but exhaustion and confusion from this vivid ordeal. But no such flight of fancy had intruded upon Henry's dreams: he lay snoring in the adjacent cot. Ford had to shake him awake for the start of the new day, and he suspected that the marshal had been back on the whiskey.

In the morning, after coffee, Henry inspected and cleaned his handgun with meticulous care, testing the action by cocking and pulling the trigger against each empty chamber. He then removed all the ammunition from his belt, cleaned and replaced each round.

At mid-morning he went to the post office to check for any messages from Washington, but there were none. Just before midday he had a lunch of beans and cornbread, saying he didn't expect to eat again until the following day. Then, not long after noon, he thanked the sheriff and explained that

Ford would leave the following day. The sheriff seemed to accept the plan without question, which made Ford think that it must have been a usual procedure in such matters for a sheriff to leave his deputy behind when going off to confront three armed offenders.

Henry's departure from Georgetown, for the ten-mile journey to Round Rock, took place without ceremony and consisted of no more than a simple handshake and nod, along with the words, 'I'll see you in Round Rock tomorrow. Go straight to the sheriff's office.'

Ford just said, 'I'll be there,' and watched from the porch of the sheriff's office as Henry departed. But for some reason he just couldn't take his eyes off the figure of the big man, straight-backed, riding at a walking pace as he rolled a cigarette, until he had passed out of sight.

Ford stayed around the sheriff's office and offered to help with any chores, but the tasks that needed doing all related to office or police procedures of which he knew nothing, so he took to sweeping the floor, then attending to the sheriff's stables, which were at the back of the office. He was told that his efforts were appreciated but he knew they were just menial tasks and of little consequence to the sheriff or his deputies.

That evening, fearing that he would have another fitful night of dreams about the preacher and his sons, he set about keeping himself busy. He attended to personal housekeeping matters, cleaning his saddle, boots, pistol and rifle. When he did retire, however, he had no need to worry as he quickly fell asleep and slept soundly.

When saddling his horse after breakfast the next day, he overheard the stall-hand talking to the stable manager. The hand was an old black man who had seen two riders with three horses pass through Georgetown in a hurry, well before first light. They had stopped to water their horses and fill water canteens. The younger of the two men looked sickly, he said, while the older one seemed agitated and was calling on his companion to be stout of heart. The stable manager was dismissive of the story and told the old man to get on with cleaning out the stall vacated by Ford's horse.

Ford left for Round Rock around mid-morning and by midday he had less than four miles to go. The familiar countryside, which he had known since he was a child, now, for some unknown reason, seemed different and as if he was seeing it for the very first time. This feeling came with a small sense of foreboding, which pushed away any homecoming joy, so he did his best to put it from his mind.

He watered his horse on the outskirts of town and had an urge to check his pistol as he stood by his horse. This he did, along with several practice goes at drawing his handgun from its holster. Each time the pistol drew with ease but these dry runs made him feel self-conscious and he kept looking around, concerned that someone might be watching.

As he rode into town, down past the past the general store towards the sheriff's office, Ford couldn't help but keep looking over his shoulder, concerned that he might be set upon by the preacher and his sons. He arrived at the sheriff's office with some little relief, only to find it closed. As he looked around for a place to sit and wait, out of the way and with his back to the wall, a neat Negro man in a brown derby said, 'The sheriff and the deputies are all over at the undertaker's. I think they may be some time. There was a shooting here last night.'

Ford felt his mouth dry. 'How many killed?' he asked.

'Three,' said the man crisply, 'and all stone dead.'

34

THE BODIES

Ford rode across to the undertaker's on Leadbetter Street but waited outside in the hope that Henry would appear with the sheriff. But nobody came out and nobody entered, and, though the front door was ajar, the large brown building seemed to be empty of life. He waited patiently for nearly twenty minutes before he pushed open the door and slowly walked into the office to stand by the empty counter. To the left was a door and it, too, was ajar.

'Hello,' he called. 'Hello, anyone there?' But there was no answer.

He walked quietly to the door as if in a church and pushed it open, slowly. He was ready to call again when he heard footsteps and voices at the far end of the long corridor. Then four men crowded into the narrow passageway and started to walk towards him. Ford immediately snatched the hat from his head.

The man leading the group, short and bald, looked up at Ford. 'Yes, can I help you?'

'I'm here to see US Marshal Henry Owens, is he here?'

All four men stopped abruptly. 'Yes,' said the first man and immediately began to roll down the shirtsleeve on his right arm. 'Yes he is.'

Ford could now clearly see the other three men, all much taller and all three wearing silver stars.

The second man, the older of the sheriffs, with a stern look, fixed his sight on Ford. 'And you? Who would you be to Marshal Owens?' His voice had authority.

Ford seemed to stumble with his reply, casting his eyes down to the floor as he searched for the right words. He glanced up to the last two men in the hallway who were now leaning to each side of the narrow corridor to get a good view of him. 'Olford Tate, I'm from here, Round Rock but I'm also Henry's deputy. We came together from Sedalia, Missouri. He told me to wait with the sheriff of Georgetown, then follow him in today.'

'Oh, I see.' The sheriff's voice changed and was softer. 'Well, I better take you to see the marshal.' He glanced over his shoulder. 'You boys go back to the office, I'll follow once I've done here.'

The two deputies squeezed past the sheriff and nodded to Ford as they passed, while the small man rolled down his other shirtsleeve, then turned to pursue the sheriff back down the hall. Ford followed after the two men, the sound of their boots noisy within the confines of the long narrow passageway, before they entered into a large dim silent room.

Against the back wall, on the far side of the open area, were three coffins upon trestles with the narrow ends pointing towards him.

Ford glanced around for Henry, expecting to see his tall figure looking down upon the men he had killed but he was nowhere to be seen. At the back of the room was a closed door; which Ford guessed was hiding Henry.

'Marshal Owens is the one on the left,' said the short man.

Ford glanced at the coffin to the left and immediately felt as if his whole body had lifted from the ground. He could no longer feel his feet against the floor and his fingers seemed numb against the brim of his hat. 'Henry?' he said from quivering lips.

He felt a hand upon his shoulder. It was the sheriff and it seemed to push him gently back to the ground. 'I guess this is a great shock?'

Ford nodded, not wanting to speak as he felt the tears starting to well in his eyes.

'He got one of them, there in the middle.' The sheriff tilted his head towards the coffin next to Henry's. 'We think it is Jonah Hayes but maybe you can advise on that. And we think he may have wounded his brother, Joshua.'

'I've never seen any of the Hayes,' said Ford as he glanced towards the third coffin. 'And that one?'

'We don't know. We think just a bystander who got hit by a stray bullet that entered his heart from a wound to the side. Bad luck for him. He just happened to be at the blacksmith's as the gunfight commenced.'

'Blacksmiths?' Ford was confused.

'Lockwood's on Ranch Road.'

Ford knew it well. 'Lockwood's? Was Mr Lockwood there?'

'He was, but he had to run for cover when the shooting started. Seems Marshal Owens followed Hayes and his two sons to Lockwood's and confronted them. It is unknown who fired first but from what Bert Lockwood has been able to tell us, the third man here may have been the first to die. He walked in through the front entrance, behind the marshal and called out. But after that it was just confusion and we have no other witnesses.'

Ford felt his heart begin to race and his breath shorten. He fought to control the discomfort and then slowly started to speak. 'But you said one was wounded?'

'Well, Bert thinks so. Some town folk saw two riders leave and one of those didn't seem to be travelling upright but bent over, clutching at his arm, high up near the shoulder.'

'So you don't have them?'

The sheriff now looked away, a little embarrassed. 'No we don't.'

'They shot a US marshal and ran away?' asked Ford his voice a little stronger.

The sheriff now turned his gaze back on to Ford. 'It wasn't exactly like that. We know the gunfight went on for some little time. It may not have been seen but it was heard. We have some people saying they counted well over thirty shots before the firing ceased, and my deputies have identified over two dozen bullet strikes against the barn walls and the stonework around the forge. We think Hayes and his wounded son may have been inside the building for some twenty minutes before they left on three horses riding north. It looks like they tried to take a wagon but in the end they left on horseback, leaving the body of this one behind.' The sheriff looked back at the middle coffin, where one of the Hayes boys now lay with his hands folded across his crotch.

'How was Henry killed?'

The sheriff didn't seem to want to answer, so the bald under-taker stepped forward clasping his hands.

'He was shot a number of times.'

'How many times?' asked Ford.

'Six, all to the chest and stomach.' He then lowered his head. 'Would you like to see him now?'

The question took Ford by surprise and he could feel his eyes widen, but he nodded. 'Yes, I guess so.' He stepped forward on stiff legs towards the unlined rough wooden casket to look at Henry, all the time hoping that this was nothing more than a terrible mistake. But through glassy eyes he saw that it was Henry, lying peacefully on his back with his eyes closed and his hair pushed back.

'It was a rotten thing they done,' said the sheriff. 'Never seen anything like it and I don't know why they did it.'

'They were wanted for killing a federal judge,' said Ford.

'I know. The marshal told me when he met with me yester-day. But still to do that—'

Ford's eyes were fixed on Henry's face as he interjected. 'They were killers.'

'I know. But' – the sheriff was shaking his head – 'to cut off his hands like that. All the years I've been in the law and I've never seen anything like it.'

'Hands,' said Ford. 'Hands?' He looked down over Henry's

body, over his big chest to his arms that lay by his side, down to the sleeves, his gaze following each fold of the fabric to the wrist. 'Good God,' he heard himself say as his eyes registered that each shirt cuff was empty.

35

HENRY'S STAR

Ford sat in the sheriff's office, the coffee going cold in his hands, while his mind raced in circles like an out-of-control fairground carousel, spinning with images of Henry, walking and talking, alive and dead, with and without hands.

'I guess you will want to speak to Bert Lockwood,' said the sheriff.

Ford was jolted from his jumbled thoughts and back to stark reality. 'Sorry?'

'I expect that you'll want to interview Bert Lockwood, the blacksmith who was there at the shooting. To hear what he has to say before you go after the Hayes.'

Ford was still confused; he shifted in his chair, spilling some coffee to the floor, as he opened his mouth to question the sheriff again. But the sheriff had turned to a deputy standing by the counter. 'Stan, you want to take the US deputy marshal over to Bert's and introduce him?'

As Ford heard the words US deputy marshal, it took him by surprise, but he did his best to hide it. 'I know Mr Lockwood,' he said, speaking up. 'I grew up here.'

'Been away long?' asked the sheriff.

'I left for cattle work in Waco three and half years ago, then went north to Missouri on a drive. I met Henry when I shot Zachary Hayes.'

'So,' said the sheriff. 'It was you who killed Zachary Hayes? I read about that. They said the man who did it was from Round Rock but the name wasn't familiar.'

'My name is Olford. The people around Round Rock know me as Ollie. Ollie Tate. Not Ford.'

The sheriff nodded his head to show that he accepted the explanation. 'Me, I'm from San Antonio myself. Only been here a year.' He drank the last of his coffee and as he placed the empty tin cup upon the edge of the desk, he said, 'And now you have unfinished business.'

'Unfinished business?' repeated Ford.

'Two down but two to go.'

Ford was still puzzled as to what the sheriff was getting at.

'Well, you will be doing a good turn to rid our state of the likes of those Hayes.' The sheriff pulled the cup back a little from the edge of the desk.

'You ready to go?' asked the deputy.

Ford looked up, questioning with his eyes.

'Ready to go and speak to Bert Lockwood. I can take you over, if you want.' The deputy gestured with his head towards the door.

'No. No, I know Mr Lockwood,' Ford repeated slowly. 'I'll go over myself.'

As Ford stood up the sheriff opened the drawer of his desk and pulled out a small coloured tin box without a lid. 'I have the marshal's personal belongings. Not much. His gun and belt were missing. I presume it was taken by one of the Hayes. I have his tobacco pouch, and of course, his badge.' The sheriff took the star from the box and held it out to Ford. 'I notice you aren't displaying yours either. I took this from his pocket. I guess you boys do that, when you're chasing down men of this disposition. Keep your identity to yourself, so you can get up close to them.'

Ford took Henry's star. 'I don't have one to wear.'

'Well, best you wear that one when you speak to Bert Lockwood. People respond better when they see authority.'

Ford rubbed his thumb over the smooth metal. 'Yes, I'll do that.'

Bert Lockwood didn't remember Ford at first glance, but he did as soon as he heard the name, Olford Tate.

'Ollie. Celia's brother,' Ford had said to help jog his memory.

'Of course,' said Bert, studying Ford's face. 'Young Ollie.' His gaze kept searching. 'You've changed somewhat.'

Ford put his hand to the scar on his cheek.

Bert looked down at the star on his chest. 'And come up in the world, too.'

Ford felt self-conscious. 'It says marshal but I'm only a deputy. This is the star of the man who was shot here. That's what I've come to ask you about.'

'You wearing his star?' It was half a statement and half a question.

Ford went to answer but the blacksmith kept talking.

'I like that. A sign of respect.'

'Are you happy to talk to me, Mr Lockwood?'

'Of course I am, Marshal. I will help all I can because you have a hard row ahead of you, I suspect, if you are to catch these two. So how do we do this?'

Ford's mind started to race again as he searched for an answer. Then he thought; how might Henry do this? 'Well,' he said, 'you talk and I'll listen.'

The blacksmith took in a deep breath, then rubbed each hand down over his leather apron before he stepped forward to begin. 'I was over here attending to the three men that the sheriff says are called Hayes, but they introduced themselves by the name of Murphy: a preacher and his two sons. He, the preacher that is, did all the talking; his two boys were mute the whole time. He said that they had come all the way down from Kansas and all their horses, five of them, needed new shoes. It was almost done when your marshal came in through the doors. I always leave both doors wide open to let in the light, but he didn't have a badge on like you, not that it would have mattered, the sun was behind him, real bright, so he was hard to see. We all looked up but paid little notice, I thought he was just another customer, but he just stood there. Then one of the preacher's boys started to get agitated. He kept looking up at the door and fidgeting, so I called out: "Can I help you?" But he just stood there in the middle of the doorway, absolutely still. It was hard to see his face from the glare of the sunlight, and I was going to walk over when a second man, about your age, leading his horse, walked in behind the marshal and said: "I got here at last", or "I'm here at last", or something like that. Then the marshal called out real loud: "Preacher, prepare to meet your maker", and then it just went crazy. The preacher and his two boys drew their guns and began firing, and the marshal began firing back, I was lucky to get out alive, I can tell you. And the noise, I couldn't hear myself think. How I never got shot I'm blessed if I know.' The blacksmith was shaking his head.

'Where did you go? Did you go and get the sheriff?'

'I sure did.'

'Straight away?' asked Ford.

'No,' said the blacksmith, shaking his head again. 'No, I went for cover like any man would do under the circumstances.'

'Of course,' said Ford. He looked around the barn at the telltale sign of the battle. 'I don't know how anyone got out of here alive.'

The blacksmith now nodded his head vigorously. 'Neither do I and I was just outside the backdoor, hold up behind the charcoal bins, but I could still see what was going on. Some of those bullets came straight through the wall, over my head, I had to get down low but I could still see and hear what was going on through the gap under the door. Lord, what a ruckus!'

'But you were able to get the sheriff? Is that when you found Marshal Owens dead?'

'Found three dead,' he said. 'But not all lying where they fell. The marshal's body had been dragged to the front of the bins and that's where they did it.'

'Did it?' repeated Ford.

'Chopped off his hands. You can see. There was an awful lot of blood. Most of it has been soaked up in the dirt but an awful lot of blood.'

Ford looked over at the dark stain on the earthen floor. 'I can't see no axe?'

'Didn't use an axe. They used the coal shovel.' The blacksmith made an up-and-down motion to mimic the blade of the shovel being thrust vertically to the ground.

Ford felt light-headed as a wave of nausea passed over him. 'Why?' he said, but the question was unanswered by the blacksmith. He was too busy telling his story.

'I was still watching when one of them yelled out: "We got them, the ones in the gazettes. The ones in the illustration. The ones that got our Zac." '

The words gripped at Ford's fuzzy mind as he recalled the photographs and illustration taken of him in Sedalia.

'Then,' said the blacksmith, 'the preacher said: "Is it the marshal with the missing finger?" And one of his boys said: "Yes it is Pa." '

'Then what happened?' Ford was fighting to keep up with the disjointed account of the gunfight by the eager witness.

'The marshal was down but he wasn't dead. He propped himself up on one elbow and' – Bert was holding his hand up as if to point a pistol – 'he fired and shot one of the preacher's boys dead. He started yelling out, calling them snakes and things and then he shot the second one but he didn't kill him. I knew he was hit though, the young one let off a yelp like a dog being kicked by a mule.'

'And then?'

'And then the preacher walked over to the marshal and I heard five or six shots, then no more. I lay there thinking: am I next? I tell you I was a worried man. Then, the preacher saw to his sons before he told the wounded one to help him drag the marshal's body over near the forge, and that's when I saw him do it, cut off the marshal's hands with the blade of the shovel. I took off over the back fence to get the sheriff. When we came back the preacher and his wounded boy was gone. That's when we got to see the marshal.' The blacksmith was looking down at his own large, blackened hands as he shook his head. 'Rattlesnakes he had said. That's what the marshal had called them and that's what they are. He is no preacher. No sir. He's a rattlesnake.'

'I don't understand,' said Ford. 'The preacher just walked up to the marshal and shot him dead. Just like that?'

The blacksmith was still looking at his hands before he let them drop to his sides. 'The marshal's gun must have been empty, but we'll never know, cos it was taken. But maybe that's all he needed, just one more bullet to finish the job.'

36

SNAKE-HUNTING

'Well, I've advised Austin of the death of a US Marshal and they have sent a response, of sorts.' The sheriff gave a dispirited wave of his hand, which held the returned telegraph. 'I've also told them that those responsible left town heading north, and I've sent telegraphs to the sheriffs of Georgetown, Waco, Hillsboro, Fort Worth and Red River Station.'

'They are well past Georgetown,' said Ford. 'Two men passed through there this morning just before dawn on three horses. It was the preacher and his wounded son.'

'You saw them?' The sheriff's face showed his puzzlement.

'No, but I was told by someone who did. It didn't add up, till now,' said Ford. 'But the sheriff in Waco should be able to apprehend them.'

The sheriff shuffled his feet. 'That's the problem.' He waved the yellow telegraph in the air again. 'He can report on their whereabouts, if he sees them, but at the moment he can't force an apprehension.'

'Why not?' Ford's voice was sharp.

'Austin City see this as a federal matter and are holding off for Washington to make the call.'

'Call? What's to call? There is already a federal apprehension order on all of the Hayes,' said Ford. 'Reward, too.'

'So I'm told,' said the sheriff. 'But I don't have a copy of the papers and nor did your marshal when I spoke to him yesterday. Do you?'

Ford shook his head with disbelief. 'So they can run free to the state line then cross over into Indian Territory?' There was no hiding the anger in Ford's voice.

'Look, this is just politics, that's all. It will fix itself in a day or two, maybe three. Once Washington tips its hat to Texas and formally asks the governor for help, he will authorize the arrest warrants and hand them over to the Rangers.' He then repeated: 'It is just the argy-bargy of politics, that's all.'

Ford could feel his temper rising at the absurdity of this state of affairs. Then, as if Henry were standing by his side with his hand upon his shoulder, Ford felt a calm come over him. 'There must be a way,' he said, as if talking to Henry. 'Something we can do?'

The sheriff lifted his shoulders. 'Well, no one can stop you from chasing them down. You're a federal deputy. You can do what you like.' He glanced at Ford's chest. 'You have the

140

authority that's vested in that badge of office.'

'But they have a day's start.' Ford looked down at the floor as he spoke, mulling over the sheriff's words.

'One is wounded and they have a lot of ground to cover.'

The proposal lifted Ford's spirits with the prospects of a solution, while the reality of what was involved pulled him down towards despair. Ford's head began to spin as the brief feeling of calmness slipped away, fast. 'Once they cross the Red River, they could head in any direction, to Kansas or Missouri.'

The sheriff shrugged his shoulders. 'That's two hundred and fifty miles away. They have to get there first.'

'I've got two good horses but no more provisions.' Ford's voice was uncertain as he said, 'I would need—'

The sheriff cut in. 'I can give you an extra horse and you only need enough provisions to get you between posts. It will allow you to travel light and fast. I'll telegraph ahead so that the district sheriffs expect you. But you will have to sign for the horse and it can't leave the state. That's the rules. You can take it as far as Red River, but then you will have to hand it over to Sheriff Munroe. With any luck you will have caught up with them by then.'

A voice from deep within seemed to be whispering, *Damn rattlesnakes.* Was it Henry, from beyond the grave? 'I'll sign,' said Ford.

'When do you want to get away? It'll be dark soon. Do you want to leave tomorrow?'

'No,' said Ford firmly. 'I want to be in Waco by this time tomorrow.'

The sheriff turned quickly to his deputies with a wide grin. 'Boys, let's give the US deputy marshal all the help he needs. He's going snake-hunting.'

141

37

RIDING FOR HENRY

Ford made Waco by last light the following day. The sheriff had received the telegraph from the sheriff at Round Rock advising of his journey, but none from Austin with the authorization to arrest two men travelling under the names of either Murphy or Hayes. But he was able to report that two men with three horses had been seen passing through the outskirts of the town; however, these details were sketchy.

'When?' asked Ford.

The sheriff seemed a little lost. 'Not sure; this morning sometime, early when it was still dark, but it may not have been them.'

'One is wounded,' said Ford. 'Any report of a wounded man seeking aid?'

'No,' said the sheriff. 'I have no other news, but I can give you a meal and place to rest for the night.'

'The meal I'll take and the horses need to be fed and watered but as for rest, that will have to wait, I want to be in Fort Worth by tomorrow night.'

The sheriff raised his eyebrows, but it went unnoticed by Ford as he turned to depart for the stables to attend to his horses.

The weather over that first night's ride had proved to be kind, with a light following breeze and a temperature that required no more that a collar to be turned up in the early hours. But the ease of the first twenty-four hours in the saddle was now fading, as dark clouds billowed on the horizon to the north like tall towers towards the heavens.

During that second night Ford rode the horses at a walk, covering three miles an hour, but as soon as it was light enough to see the trail clearly, he increased this to four miles an hour, giving an overall average of three and half miles an hour. But in practical terms it worked out to be just a little over three, with lost time for watering of the horses and changing mounts. This reality meant that he didn't make Fort Worth until close to midnight after nearly thirty hours in the saddle, and the journey was now starting to take its toll. His shoulder felt stiff and his back ached, but it was the bleeding that worried him the most. It was getting worse, causing him to change pads daily, something he had never had to do before now. He also felt light-headed and constantly thirsty, which he mistakenly put down only to a lack of sleep.

The sheriff at Fort Worth was surprised to see him when he was woken from his bed by the duty deputy. 'I heard you were coming and travelling hard,' he said to Ford. 'But I didn't expect to see you for another day.'

Ford was dismissive of what he considered small talk. 'Have you seen them?' he asked.

'No,' said the sheriff, 'nor have I heard a word. Do you think that maybe you passed them? They may not be travelling at night like you. Easy to pass someone by if they have camped overnight.'

'I don't think so. They will want to get away after shooting a US marshal' – Ford licked his dry lips – 'but I really don't know, so I have to push on. If I am in front, then I'll get them when they go to cross the Red River. But if they cross before me, I'll never catch them.'

The sheriff, a man about the age of Henry and with silver in his cropped hair, conceded Ford's point with a nod. 'But you don't plan to go on, straight away, do you?'

'Why not?'

'Well you look, well . . .' He paused as his eyes searched Ford's face. 'You look all in.'

'I'm fine,' said Ford. 'If I can feed the horses and maybe get something to eat myself. . . ?'

'Sure,' said the sheriff. 'Do you want to wash up?'

Ford cupped the water to his face; it felt fresh and clean as he closed his eyes and let it soothe his skin. He then rubbed soap over his neck, the water falling brown and gritty back into the bowel. He bought more water to his face and could feel the raised scar on his cheek, slightly tender against his thumb; then, as he lifted his face and looked into the mirror he received a shock. The man staring back at him was old, gaunt and tired. 'Is that you, Ollie?' he could hear himself say as he gazed at his whiskered growth and scar. But it was his eyes that he noticed the most, they seemed cold and unyielding, as if he were looking at another man – one he had never met before. *What's happening?* he thought; *What's happening to me?*

Ford had planned to leave Forth Worth within the hour but he stayed till just before first light, falling into a deep sleep for nearly five hours, after the sheriff had persuaded him to rest. 'Red River is one hundred miles from here,' he had said, 'and you won't be able to do that without resting somewhere, be it Decatur or Bowie, but I doubt if you will make it to the grass-lands before you fall off your horse.' Ford wasn't convinced until the sheriff added: 'And what sort of condition are you going to be in when you do catch up with these killers? You need to be on your game, not so exhausted that you can't hold a gun straight.'

But when Ford woke he didn't feel rested. His body ached all over and he had a splitting headache that lasted halfway to Decatur. Relief came only when he was watering the horses from a deep creek that allowed him to completely submerge his head after he had taken a long drink.

He made Decatur an hour before last light to hear the news from the sheriff that two men with three horses had purchased provisions from a smallholding to the west, just two to three miles from town.

'When?' asked Ford.

'Just this morning,' said the sheriff. 'They were polite, paid a good price for some salted beef and feed for the horses and gave the name Murphy. They also bought a pickle jar.'

'How are they travelling?'

'They're travelling hard like you, but one of them, the younger one, is not too well. His arm is in a sling.'

'So where would they be now?'

'My guess is that they will be just past Bowie by now.'

'How far?'

'Bowie is thirty miles, with another thirty to Red River Station.'

'Just thirty miles from Red River; that means they will cross over into Indian country tomorrow. Have you a telegraph from Austin City authorizing the apprehension of two men travelling under the name of Hayes or Murphy?'

The sheriff shook his head. 'Nope. All I got was a telegraph advising that a US deputy marshal was chasing two men who were wanted on a federal order. But they must have got that wrong, because I see that you are a marshal, not a deputy marshal.' The sheriff was looking at Henry's star.

'They killed the marshal who wore this badge and we were partners, so I am now riding for him.'

The sheriff nodded his head in acknowledgement then said, 'So this is personal, then?'

'As it can get,' said Ford.

'I can understand that,' said the sheriff, as he put his hand on Ford's shoulder and it felt like Henry's familiar touch.

38

FLOODING

During the ride that night Ford could see the flashes of distant lightning upon the coiled pillars of cloud. He guessed that it was raining somewhere to the north but exactly how far ahead he couldn't tell. But when he passed through Bowie, two hours before first light, he could smell the rain and by the time he was able to sight the thin line of the horizon, he knew he was in for some stormy weather.

The cloud was as black as charcoal when the downpour swept in from the north-east some forty minutes later on the tail of a strong wind. Ten minutes on and he was wet through and having trouble seeing as the large heavy drops hit and stung his face.

By his reckoning he was now twenty-five miles from Red River on a waterlogged track. The stabbing blade of panic piercing at his gut was telling him that he was too late, that the preacher and his wounded son had already crossed into the Indian Territories. And with this rain he would have no chance of following their tracks, no matter how recently they had been made. Once they crossed the state line, he knew, they would be beyond his reach.

On the final leg, the last ten miles into the station, Ford had slowed to a crawl with the horses sliding on the mud and rocks that washed along the trail. In a small depression he stopped and walked the horses through a narrow but fast-running creek. As he looked back he realized it was the place where he and Henry had caught up with the muleskinners but the familiar surroundings now seemed different. It was not just because of their waterlogged state, but that his recollection seemed to come from a distant and hazy past.

When at last he arrived at Red River Station it was late in the afternoon, with the sky still gloomy and rain misting on a light breeze as the water drained in flowing streams down the centre of the street. When he got to the sheriff's office he found it closed, with a sign saying BACK IN FIVE MINUTES. When five minutes passed, then another five, then another five again, he went looking and found the clean, dry lawman sucking on candy in the general store.

Ford extended his hand but Munroe didn't offer his in return, only saying, 'I heard you were coming back.'

'Have you seen them? The preacher and his son, travelling under the name of Murphy?'

Munroe was casually leaning back against the counter; he nodded silently as he made a sucking sound on the sweet toffee.

'When?' asked Ford.

Munroe looked Ford up and down. 'I saw what was done to those muleskinners. They've been held up here, being treated for their wounds. Both are only just well enough to travel again. They are heading up north to Stillwater.' He looked Ford up and down again. 'I just can't believe anyone could do such a thing to two old men.'

Ford dismissed the comment. 'Marshal Henry Owens is dead,' he said. 'It was the preacher and his son who did it and they are wanted on a federal warrant. I need to apprehend them before they cross the river.'

'Well,' said Munroe, 'that's what you say, but unless you can show me a copy of the federal warrant, I don't believe you. I met the preacher and I believe him to be a man of the Lord.'

Ford could feel his temperature rising. 'I need to apprehend them before they cross the Red River,' he said again.

'Well, for that I believe you are too late. I reckon they'll be crossing the river right now.'

147

Ford could now feel the anger like fire in his blood. He stepped forward, his eyes fixed on the sheriff and as he did he saw a flash of alarm on Munroe's face. 'Well, you pray to the good Lord that I get the preacher and his son, because if I don't I'll come after you, to hold you to account for failing to do your duty.'

The sheriff straightened up and opened his mouth to speak but nothing came out except for the candy that rolled from his lips and dropped to the floor.

The shopkeeper observed the sheriff's nervousness and smirked before giving a soft chuckle.

Ford turned to leave.

'You . . .' the sheriff said with a cough.

Ford turned back. 'Yes?'

'You – you need to show some respect.'

'For what? You're supposed to be the law but all I see is someone who won't get involved.' Ford turned back towards the door and began to walk.

The shopkeeper chuckled again.

'Well, at least I don't go cutting ears off old men,' called the sheriff in his own defence.

Ford stopped in the doorway, his silhouette framed by the grey light, his hand resting on the grip of his pistol. He turned his head. 'No, that is something you would never do.' He turned side-on, back towards the sheriff. 'But then I doubt if you'd do anything to anyone no matter how far they were on the wrong side of the law. You're a fence-sitter and fence-sitters do nothing wrong and nothing right.'

The shopkeeper let out a cackle.

The sheriff coughed. 'You—'

But it was too late. Ford had gone.

The two-mile ride to the crossing was done at a gallop. Ford left the other two horses behind in an attempt to catch up to the preacher and his son before they crossed the river. If I don't, he told himself, this will be a lost cause. So he pushed his tired horse to its limits, its hoofs splashing and spraying water high as he leant forward in the saddle. He rode hard with his right hand touching the butt of his revolver from time to time, to push it into the holster; his palm felt the cold but comforting grip of the Peacemaker. It was a grim reminder of what lay ahead, of what he must be prepared to do: to confront and kill the preacher and his son.

But how? The touch of his hand upon the smooth iron had triggered a chilling sense of reality, the realization of why he had pushed himself so hard in the pursuit of these two men who had killed and mutilated Henry. But now what? He had no plan. He didn't even know what they looked like. Did the preacher dress in black? How would he identify them? But, more important, how would he kill them? Should he shoot them as soon as he knew it was them? Should he wait until they were together? Should he identify himself first?

Ford kept riding hard and was now nearing the river but he needed time to think. What would Henry do? *Think*, he told himself. Should he ride up with his gun drawn? *Think*. Should he stop short and approach on foot? *Think*.

The river was now coming into view between the patches of brush along the bank, and as he eased his horse down from the gallop he saw two men not more than thirty yards away and slightly to the left, standing, one pointing to the far bank. Were they his quarry? One turned; Ford touched his hand to his revolver. He could now see their horses a little further away to the left. Just two horses. He was almost upon them when the other man turned, waved and smiled. Ford brought his horse to a halt.

'You won't be able to jump this one, she's still flooding,' called the man, the smile of Texas humour still upon his lips. 'It's flowing high, wide and handsome today.'

'Yes,' said Ford, his mind racing.

'We won't be attempting a crossing today,' the man added.

'No,' said Ford, 'I guess not.'

The older man, still pointing to the other side, said to his companion. 'We'll hold the mob close and be ready to go. This rain should just about be done by tonight. Then we can cross maybe in a day or two after that.'

'More like three,' said the younger man.

'We'll come out over there and move them on north without delay. I don't want any backing up or slowing us down, Dan.'

The young man with the smile agreed. 'I've got that, Mr Gill. Move 'em on quick.'

'So nobody's been crossing today?' asked Ford.

'Not swimming,' said the older man. 'Nor yesterday either. But it's starting to slow, just a little.' He set his eyes on Ford. 'And when it's down enough, we are first in line.'

'I'm not here to jump your claim on crossing, I've got no cattle to move to the other side. I was just trying to catch up with two riders heading north with three horses, before they leave Texas. Have you seen anybody like that?'

The older man looked at the star on Ford's jacket. 'They wanted?'

'Yes, sir, they are.'

The older man turned and looked at the younger man, then turned his head back to Ford. 'There are two men with three horses loading on the ferry about half a mile up river. They are keen to cross and have paid the ferryman handsome for the bother, because he wasn't keen to take them. They were also loading a muleskinners' wagon on as we came by. Why they wouldn't wait till at least tomorrow is beyond me. But now I know. They have the law on their tail.'

'I'm obliged,' said Ford, and turned his horse up river.

'What are you planning to do?' called the older man.

Ford looked over his shoulder at the two men. 'I don't know yet.' Then he rode off, his left hand unclipping Henry's star from his jacket.

39

WELCOME FRIEND

Ford sighted the outline of the wagon as it appeared and dis-appeared through the brushwood. From the saddle of his horse as he raced along the riverbank it appeared to be perched upon the water. The top of the wagon with its covered hoops was not far below the wire rope that stretched and dipped over the river from bank to bank. From this steel line hung the large block and tackle that tethered the ferry to the cable and allowed it to be pulled to the far side of the river. Ford slowed his horse to walk, eyes fixed upon the ferry that jolted from the force of the swollen river pushing against its side. A voice yelled but he couldn't make out what was being said as the rain started to fall with heavy taps upon the brim of his hat. He slid off his mount and started to walk towards the landing where a group of men were busy, preparing the flat-top barge with its cargo for the crossing.

As he got closer he could now clearly see the muleskinners' wagon balanced upon the fragile timber deck of the ferry. On the side that faced Ford was a man in black, tying off a horse to the front wagon wheel, but Ford couldn't see who else was aboard. On the bank, immediately behind the ferry, were three men, two holding long poles and fighting to keep the barge in position where a narrow plank linked the vessel to the shore.

As Ford approached the rain began to come down heavily, dimming the light to an eerie grey. When he was within two steps of the men he spoke. 'I need to get on board,' he said.

The man closest to him jumped a little. 'You surprised me.'

'I need to get on,' repeated Ford.

151

'No can do,' replied the man, his voiced raised against the noise of the downpour. 'The ferry is already overloaded and with this rain we need to move real quick. She's leaving now; this is risky enough as it is.'

Ford pulled Henry's badge from his pocket. 'I need to get on,' he said again. 'It will take but a minute for me to do what I need to.'

The ferry foreman looked at Ford and pleaded: 'My men can't hold her any longer with the load she has on board. I've got to let her go. And' – he pointed to the other side of the bank – 'they are ready to haul.'

Ford looked at the water swirling by, turning, dipping, rocking and pulling at the ferry as if to wrench it from its moorings. He could feel his fear rise and he sucked in a deep breath. 'Just let me get on,' he said. 'Then let her go.'

The foreman glanced towards his men, their backs bent as they leant in hard with their shoulders against the poles, then looked down at the star in Ford's hand. 'OK,' he said. 'But get on quick.'

Ford felt the foreman place his hand upon his back to hurry him on to the narrow gangplank, which bounced under his feet. The urge to freeze gripped him as he saw the water below his feet but it was too late: the foreman's firm hand propelled him forward; his feet were slipping on the wet timber, then in a final leap, he was aboard the ferry, just as the voice behind him yelled, 'Let her go.'

'Cast off' came the return cry and Ford felt the deck beneath his feet move and twist as the ferry began its journey out into the heaving river. He raised his arms out to his sides for balance as the rope to the cable took up the slack with a twang that shook the barge and rocked the muleskinners' wagon. Ford put out his left hand to steady himself on the wheel as he heard the scuffle of hoofs from two frightened horses on the far side of the wagon. He glanced at the water that now flowed behind him in red murky torrents, splashed by the blobs of heavy rain, and he felt his fear rise. He hung his head and gripped at the wagon wheel with both hands, tightly, while his pale lips mumbled a prayer he had learnt as a child.

He didn't see the man in the long dark coat, wet through from the rain, he just heard his voice as he said, 'Welcome aboard, friend. I'm Preacher Murphy, and who might you be?'

40

CROSSING THE JORDAN

Ford didn't look up, keeping his hands still tight on the wagon wheel as it shuddered with each frequent lurch of the ferry from the churning current.

'My name is Olford,' he said, 'but my mother always called me Ollie.'

'Well, Ollie, we cross the River Jordan together. We are but in the hands of the Lord till we reach the other side and freedom.'

'Don't you mean safety?' Ford gazed down at the rickety timber of the old deck beneath his feet.

'That too,' said the preacher. 'That too, but what brings you on board, friend? A man on foot is a rare sight. You're not planning on going far when you get to the other side?'

'No,' said Ford. 'This is as far as I plan to go.'

'Have you paid your way? This little trip has cost me and my associates a small ransom and we knew of no other passengers. Your presence may help to defray some of our costs.'

'I'm willing to pay.'

The preacher looked upon the brim of Ford's hat, which hid his face. 'How much are you willing to pay, friend?'

'What ever is necessary; name your price.'

'I will,' said the preacher, 'when we get to the other side.'

Ford kept his head down as he hung on to the wagon wheel that rocked beneath his grip and watched a pair of old worn boots come into view, to stand next to the preacher.

'You want a drink, preacher?' came the cackled voice and Ford recognized it immediately. It was Seth the muleskinner.

'A drink?' said the preacher. 'Do you think a man of the Lord should drink?'

'Suit yourself.' The muleskinner turned to go.

'Maybe one small mouthful to protect against the inclemency of the weather.'

The sound of the whiskey bottle against the preacher's lips was close to Ford's ear.

'And you, friend?' asked the preacher.

'That's my whiskey,' said Seth. 'Don't give it away.'

'I'll buy you more when we get to Stillwater.' The preacher's tone was firm. 'And this man is a paying passenger.'

Ford could feel his fear taking hold, paralysing him. With all his force he willed his right hand free from its grip on the wheel and took the whiskey bottle. As he did so, he caught sight of Henry's Colt with the letters H.O. on the grip. It hung from the muleskinner's waist along with the large knife from the Red River general store. And for just an instant it seemed as if Henry was present there with him, close by and saying in his Southern way, 'When a man still does what needs to be done, when he is scared to his back teeth, when he knows the risks, when he knows it will cause him harm, only then can it be said that he is no coward.'

Ford lifted the bottle to his lips, tilted his head back and drank. He then lowered his gaze to Seth, to look into the cruel, sunken eyes and upon the open mouth with its blackened, broken teeth, and then to the grisly sight of where his ear had been cut from his head.

The muleskinner's eyes opened wide. 'You,' he said. 'It's you.'

'You know this man?' said the preacher.

'It's him.'

'Who?' said the preacher, annoyed.

'The one with the scar. The deputy who was travelling with the marshal. The marshal with the missing finger.'

'The one with the scar?' said the preacher. He leant in close to squint at Ford. 'Are you sure?'

The muleskinner drew Henry's pistol from the holster. 'It's him all right.'

Ford looked down at the muzzle of Henry's Colt, but for some reason it didn't seem threatening, just familiar.

The muleskinner saw where Ford's eyes were fixed. 'Yeah, I got it back, didn't I? The preacher sold it to me fair and square, so it's mine for keeps.' His bony hand thrust forward and lifted Ford's Peacemaker from his holster. 'But I get this one free. I've been getting lots of prizes of late. Real good prizes.' He called out, over his shoulder. 'Quint,' There was no answer, so he called again, louder, as the rain fanned on the wind to run across the open river like a spray from a high waterfall. 'Quint, get here.'

The other muleskinner shuffled down the side of the wagon as it rocked, then shuddered. The ferry was now approaching the middle of the flooding river, the most perilous point of the voyage and the point of no return.

'Look what we've got here,' said Seth. 'These boys didn't get them both in Round Rock, like they said. Just the marshal with the missing finger, not his deputy.'

Quint peered as he wiped long wet strands of hair from his eyes and began to giggle. 'But we've got him now.'

Seth held out Ford's pistol. 'Take his gun and get the pickle jar. I want to show him what we've got.'

Quint continued to snigger as he took the pistol from Seth,

then he turned and went to the front of the wagon.

'Have we got a surprise for you. The preacher has given me and Quint a gift from the Lord in return for his poor boy to rest in our wagon on his journey to Stillwater.'

Quint returned, taking careful, slow, steps alongside the wagon as he nursed a large glass jar against his chest with his left arm. When he was just behind Seth the ferry heaved and he fell against rear wheel.

'Careful,' shouted Seth. 'Now hold it up so he can see.'

Quint eased his right hand under the jar and lifted it from where it had been cradled in his arm. He pushed it towards Ford's face.

Seth ran his hand down over the wet glass to wipe it so that Ford could see, and there, inside, upright, in a pale-yellow liquid, were two hands, upright as if praying. And one of the hands had a missing finger.

'See that,' said Seth. 'These are the hands that done this to me and Quint.' He pointed to the disfigurement on the side of his head. 'But now I've got them hands, cut off by a preacher and put in a pickle jar.'

The ferry jolted to the sound of straining rope that could be heard feeding slowly through the overhead pulleys as the ferry edged forward along the wire cable.

The preacher seemed preoccupied, rifling through his pockets, searching in a frenzy before he eventually pulled a small pistol and a folded magazine page from his pocket. Fumbling, he opened it. He squinted, eyes close to the page in the poor light, then looked up at Ford's face. 'Is that him? Are you sure? The one with the scar?'

'Ask him,' said Seth.

The preacher looked close again at Ford's face, examining him in detail. 'Did you kill my boy? My son Zachary?'

Ford held the preacher's look for a long moment before saying, 'It was me.'

'You coward. You shot my boy dead without a chance.'

156

'I gave him a chance,' said Ford, raising his voice against the sound of the heavy rain. 'All he had to do was give back to me what he had taken.'

'What had he taken? A little money? Was that reason enough to kill my boy?'

'It was not about reason; it was about choice: money or life. He chose money, so I took his life.'

'You will be damned for what you did and spend all eternity in hell.'

'If that is true I will have you and your sons for company, for killing a judge and a US marshal.'

The ferry swung to the left, then jolted hard with a thud as the rope tether took up with a sharp snap that threw all four men towards the side of the wagon. Quint fell, the wet pickle jar slipping from his hands to smash upon the timber deck, scattering glass and liquid and leaving the two pale, white hands lying palms up upon the yellow stained boards. The falling muleskinner let out a yell as he came down hard upon the broken base of the jar, a tall shard of glass slicing deep into his knee through skin and muscle, right to the bone. Seth half-turned to reach out to his wounded partner giving Ford the briefest of opportunities. Ford took it. He thrust out his hand, grasped the handle of Henry's big knife and pulled it free from the scabbard on Seth's belt.

The large silver blade flashed in the dim light just before Ford thrust the honed blade deep into the muleskinner's stomach. Seth looked up in complete surprise; his mouth was open but no sound came from his lips as he silently mouthed his disbelief. Ford pulled the knife free, the blade now dark with blood as the muleskinner fell backwards, gripping his bleeding wound, to tumble on top of his injured partner.

The barge turned, then jolted again just as a shot was fired from the preacher's small pistol. The flash lit the scene of chaos and confusion for just an instant as the bullet passed under Ford's arm to strike him in the left side, then exit to punch into the side of the large wagon, splintering wood.

Ford lunged at the pistol with Henry's knife in an attempt to stop the preacher from firing a second shot. The razor-sharp blade went in under the barrel and struck the preacher's fingers wrapped around the front of the pistol grip. He instinctively pulled his hand away but in doing so dragged his knuckles up across the fine steel edge, completely severing two of his fingers. He dropped the gun and seized at the bleeding stumps, stumbling backwards to fall upon the deck.

Ford felt his knees buckle and he had to fight to stay on his feet. He pressed a hand to his side and felt the warm flow of blood leaking from his wound as the ferry jolted again and the ropes screeched, pulling tight on to the overhead cable. Ford looked down at the knife, its blade still dark with blood as drops of rain splashed to show the silver edge. He looked over at the thick tight rope, straining as it slowly edged through the bulky pulleys, and with all his strength he swung the knife like a sabre at the hemp tether that bound them to the wire cable and the safety of the far bank.

The blade sliced through the rope, which snapped with a fierce twang that sent the running end flying through the pulleys in a spray of water and heat that drew blue smoke. The pulley-wheels spun on their axles so fast that they continued to whirl long after the rope had whipped its tail through the timber block to gain its freedom and race across the surface of the swollen river to the far bank.

Now free and at the mercy of the massive flow of the Red River, the pathetic craft began to turn slowly like a leaf caught in the eddies of a fast-flowing street drain. Its timbers creaked and buckled, the deck tilting to be washed by muddy water. The rear of the large, heavy wagon leaned precariously, then slipped sideways six or seven inches, stopped, then slid again, stopped, then again towards the fragile handrail, coming to a halt as if by divine intervention. Ford felt himself slowly collapse upon the sloping deck, to sit alongside Henry's severed hands and the now kneeling, praying preacher, whose face was white and twisted with fear.

'What have you done?' he yelled. 'What have you done?'

'Crossing the River Jordan, preacher,' said Ford as he felt the river wash over the deck and heard the steel rims of the wagon wheels slid again across the slippery timbers. 'I'm crossing the River Jordan with the rattlesnakes and the muleskinners.'

'Oh Lord,' cried the preacher as the barge tilted then quivered as if in a death throe, sending the wagon, mules and horses sliding with grinding, screeching fear from the deck and into the torrents of the Red River.

Ford closed his eyes as if to rest, the water was now washing warm over him like a blanket being drawn over a chilled and tired body. He felt no fear, no pain, just a pleasant and soothing feeling as the water spread across his legs and stomach to lap against his bleeding wound.

'The Lord will make you pay,' cried the preacher, his voice trembling with terror.

'If that is true,' said Ford, as he half-opened his sleepy eyes and felt the water rise above his chest, 'Then, so be it.'